SONARELLE

Stories That Echo

SONARELLE

Stories That Echo

Bindu Unnikrishnan

EXCELLER BOOKS®
A GLOBAL PRESS

SONARELLE
Stories That Echo

Inside illustrations by Wamia Rahman
Cover concept by Rejin Ramakrishnan
Cover design by Exceller Books

Print ISBN: 978-93-47397-38-7

Published in India in 2026 by Exceller Books,
An imprint of GE Group,
G1, Dream Apartment, Degree College Road, Belgharia,
Kolkata, 700056, India
www.excellerbooks.com

EXCELLER BOOKS®
A GLOBAL PRESS

"We are shaped not by what we hold, but by what reverberates within us. I call this Sonarelle."

– Bindu Unnikrishnan

Dedication

To the dreamers —
who imagine endlessly, feel deeply,
and live most vividly within their emotions

Acknowledgements

My foremost thanks are to the known and unknown people whose stories quietly became mine, even when I observed or experienced them from a distance. Some of these narratives are rooted in truth, gently enriched with my creative voice; others were born entirely of imagination, shaped during moments when life imposed stillness, and only the mind remained free.

I am deeply grateful to every friend who cheered me on, especially during moments when I struggled to believe in myself. They read my stories word for word, offering thoughtful insights and helping me see how each piece could grow stronger. I consider myself truly blessed, for they gave me the rarest gift of all—their time, which, by any measure, is the most precious gift one can offer.

I am indebted to my parents for a childhood filled with love, encouragement, and the confidence to trust my own voice.

My sister not only inspired me but also stood firmly beside me, rooting for me even as she carried her own struggles. From her, I learned the quiet, enduring strength of unconditional love.

My daughter made me a storyteller early in life; determined never to run out of tales for her, I kept inventing stories long after we had finished book after book.

To my husband, for patiently enduring my creative storms, my sudden silences, and my whimsical detours. Thank you for letting me disappear into my fictional worlds without complaint.

I am deeply thankful to the little powerhouse of talent, Wamia Rahman, the artist behind the illustrations, and Rejin Ramakrishnan, who painstakingly put the entire book together, meticulously attending to every detail, from the cover to the contents.

Thanks to Nyra Publishers for allowing me to include my story 'The Christmas Game', which was first published in their anthology 'Tis the Season to Be Jolly'.

Finally, I thank those who loved me consistently and stood by me like a rock. More than my words, they understood my silences.

— Bindu Unnikrishnan

Contents

Preface

I have always believed that stories do not disappear. They linger. Born in childhood or shaped in youth, they hum quietly in the background and echo long after we think we have forgotten them.

Sonarelle was born from those echoes—of a girl behind a window who showed me how loneliness imagines its own world; of a teacher whose handbag could turn the ordinary into magic; and of a grieving boy whose lost kite carried his dead father's letters from across India.

Some echoes arrived as laughter: a lazy man jolted awake by an absurd dream, a couple stumbling through a foreign holiday, two strangers in a Delhi airport discovering that missed flights sometimes take us exactly where we are meant to be.

Others came wrapped in love and longing: a mismatched couple who fit perfectly together, a forgotten love note resurfacing at the wrong time, an unanswered call that altered a life, and a wife who was understood too late.

There were echoes of women rising. Women who reclaimed the parts of themselves the world had tried to silence.

Some echoes emerged from stranger places: a red button that could take you anywhere, a mirror opening into another life, conspiracies whispering through Kerala's backwaters, Christmas magic returning to a weary heart, and worlds where humans, aliens, and accountability collided.

Finally came echoes of endings and the beginnings hidden within them: a love story unfolding across lifetimes, a Sunday breakfast stitching a couple back together, a woman entrusting her fading memories to a living diary and choosing, with courage, what to hold and what to let go.

These stories, real, imagined, dreamt, remembered, ask the same questions:

- What do we carry?
- What do we release?
- How do these echoes shape who we become?

If *Sonarelle* makes you pause, smile, ache, or remember something you thought you had forgotten, then it has fulfilled its purpose.

— Bindu Unnikrishnan

SECTION I
Childhood Echoes

1

The Girl behind the Window

Ishika had always felt invisible—a "cellophane-like" presence that people seemed to look straight through. She was neither the star student who made teachers proud nor part of the popular crowd that filled the halls with laughter and chatter.

She lingered in quiet corners—at the back of classrooms, in the dim recesses of the library, and in the silences between conversations where no one thought to include her. If she disappeared one day, no one would even notice.

Everything changed the day she found the window. It had fascinated her ever since she joined the school.

It all began as a prank, devised by the school's reigning mean girls to ensure Ishika was never allowed into their lunch group or inner circle. "You have to complete a few tasks first," declared Manisha, the most popular girl in the school, where

Ishika had recently joined after moving from the north, where her father was stationed.

There was a quiet cruelty in the lives of children whose fathers served in the military. Constant transfers meant constant goodbyes—old friends lost and new ones never truly made. For an introvert like Ishika, it was a painful cycle; each new school reminded her how difficult it was to belong.

Being part of Manisha's group was the ultimate prize. It was the circle everyone wanted to join, and Ishika desperately tried to fit in. She did everything Manisha asked, even when the tasks were a little more than thinly veiled bullying.

"There is a window somewhere in this school," Manisha said one day. "From there, you'll see a portal to another world. Find it, and you can join us."

Why did it feel different this time? Why couldn't Ishika dismiss it as just another cruel joke? What drove her to search the school every lunch break, desperately looking for that elusive window?

She knew the ache of loneliness—the longing to be seen, to be part of something, to belong.

After countless hours wandering empty hallways and finding nothing but disappointment, Ishika finally gave up. She realised she did not need anyone else to fill the silence. She was enough.

Gradually, she found peace in her solitude, learning to savour her own company. She wandered through the quiet halls, lost in daydreams, weaving stories, and humming softly to herself.

Then, one afternoon, long after she had abandoned hope, she found it.

The window was hidden deep in a forgotten wing of the school, a place even other students avoided. Teachers had warned them to stay away, muttering about termite-infested beams and crumbling ceilings. But curiosity—her only unwavering companion—led Ishika there on a dull, ordinary afternoon.

The hallway was thick with silence, as though the air itself held its breath. Dust-coated desks lay abandoned, and the scent of forgotten books lingered heavily. Cobwebs draped the corners like fragile curtains. It felt like stepping into another world.

At the very end of the hall, there was a single, solitary window.

Its frame was cracked, vines creeping over the wood as if nature itself were trying to reclaim it. The glass, though clouded with age, revealed a sight that sent a shiver down her spine.

On the other side was standing a girl.

She was wearing the same crisp school uniform—a pleated skirt swaying gently, a neatly pressed collared shirt, and the familiar emblem stitched over her chest. Her hair, braided immaculately, framed a face marked by a knowing, almost teasing smile. But it was her eyes that made Ishika forget to breathe. They did not merely meet her gaze; they reached into her, searching, recognizing—as if they had been waiting all along.

A shiver ran through Ishika's spine. Her pulse thundered in her ears as she took a hesitant step forward, her breath fogging against the cold glass.

The girl tilted her head, her voice slicing through the silence as if the barrier between them did not exist.

"Hi. I'm Meghna. I was wondering when you'd finally notice me."

The first time Ishika spoke to Meghna, she was not sure whether she was awake or trapped in some strange dream.

That night, sleep eluded her. She lay tangled in her sheets, replaying their eerie yet strangely familiar conversation. Meghna had spoken with unsettling certainty, as though she had known Ishika forever. But that was impossible—wasn't it?

Yet, when lunch break arrived the next day, Ishika found herself hurrying back to the abandoned corridor, a nervous excitement tingling in her fingertips.

She hesitated before the window, her heart pounding. What if Meghna wasn't there? What if she had imagined everything?

Then, as if she had been waiting, Meghna appeared.

"Back so soon?" she grinned, leaning lazily against the windowsill. "Missed me already?"

"I—I don't even know you," Ishika stammered.

Meghna placed a hand over her heart, feigning injury. "Ouch. That hurts."

Ishika studied her carefully—the same braided hair, the same uniform, the same amused expression, as though she knew a secret Ishika did not.

"Who are you?" Ishika asked.

Meghna sighed dramatically. "Didn't we cover this yesterday? I'm Meghna."

"But I've never seen you before—not in class, not in the corridors, nowhere."

Meghna smirked. "Maybe you weren't looking hard enough."

That made no sense. Ishika noticed everything.

Trying to change the subject, she asked, "Why do you always stand at this window?"

Meghna shrugged. "Why do you always come back?"

That was a fair question.

"I don't know," Ishika admitted.

Meghna's grin widened. "Then let's call it fate."

Ishika narrowed her eyes. Meghna was strange, but undeniably intriguing. Something about her felt magnetic—as though she had always existed in the unnoticed spaces of Ishika's life.

Over the next few days, their conversations became routine. Ishika slipped away during lunch, and Meghna was always there, waiting.

They talked about everything—school, teachers, the absurdity of homework, and the undeniable tragedy of Monday mornings. Meghna had an opinion on everything, and she delivered them with effortless humour.

"Why don't you ever eat lunch?" Ishika asked one day, chewing her sandwich.

Meghna waved a dismissive hand. "Too much chewing. I prefer to conserve my energy for being fabulous."

Ishika laughed. "That makes no sense."

"Neither does your obsession with chocolate, but here we are."

"You wear the same uniform every day," Ishika pointed out.

Meghna smirked. "Unlike you, I've mastered minimalism."

Ishika frowned. "Where do you go after lunch?"

For the first time, Meghna's smile faltered.

She tilted her head, studying Ishika as though weighing a decision. Then, in a quieter voice, she said, "Some questions are better left unanswered. Not every door is meant to be opened, Ishika. Are you sure you want to step through this one?"

A chill crept up Ishika's spine.

"Why?" she whispered.

Meghna's eyes darkened, their warmth vanishing like a candle blown out. "Because once you know the answer, you can't unlearn it."

The words hung heavy in the air, pressing down between them.

For the first time since meeting Meghna, Ishika felt something unfamiliar take hold of her – Fear.

Ishika had never been good at letting things go. She was the kind of person who reread messages to uncover hidden meanings, who could not sleep without knowing the ending of a half-watched film, and who needed answers to things that did not make sense.

And Meghna did not make sense.

That night, Ishika lay awake, replaying their conversation.

Why did she say – *Some questions are better left unanswered.*

Who was Meghna? Where did she go after lunch? Why was she always at that window—and nowhere else?

The next afternoon, as soon as the bell rang, Ishika bolted toward the abandoned wing, her heart pounding in sync with her hurried footsteps.

Meghna was already there, arms folded, a knowing smirk playing on her lips.

"You're early," she teased. "Did you miss me, or just run out of patience?"

Ishika did not bother to reply. She strode straight to the window, her eyes blazing with determination.

"Tell me the truth, Meghna."

The smirk wavered. "I always do."

"No," Ishika pressed, her voice edged with frustration. "You dodge my questions. You never tell me anything about yourself. Where do you go after lunch? Why is this the only place I ever find you? Why does no one else ever mention you?"

Meghna's gaze sharpened, the playful glint in her eyes darkening.

"Stop."

Ishika hesitated. "Stop what?"

Meghna sighed, shaking her head as if Ishika had shattered something fragile. "You're ruining it."

"Ruining what?"

Meghna leaned in, pressing her palms against the windowsill. When she spoke, her voice was low and measured, laced with an ominous tone.

"I like you, Ishika. But if you keep asking these questions, I will disappear. And you will never see me again."

Ishika's breath caught in her throat. She did not know why those words unsettled her so deeply, but they did.

For a long moment, neither of them spoke.

Meghna exhaled. Then, more softly, she said, "Let me stay."

It was not a plea; it was a choice. Ishika could either press for the truth or keep Meghna in her life—but not both.

Ishika swallowed and slowly nodded.

Meghna's smile returned, lazy and triumphant. "Good girl."

Ishika narrowed her eyes. "So now I have to follow your rules?"

Meghna grinned. "Exactly. Rule number one: no more questions about me."

Ishika sighed. "Fine."

Meghna clapped her hands. "Great! Now tell me, did that boring history teacher put you to sleep again?"

And just like that, the conversation shifted back to their usual banter. But something was different now—a new layer of unspoken understanding, a secret bargain. Deep inside, Ishika knew she had just made a deal she might regret.

Numbers hated Ishika, and the feeling was mutual. She had tried to understand math—she really had—but equations twisted themselves into unreadable hieroglyphics, formulas blurred into meaningless gibberish, and word problems felt like riddles designed to humiliate her.

So when the math teacher announced a surprise test, Ishika knew she was doomed.

That afternoon, she stormed into the abandoned wing, scowling. Meghna, as always, was waiting at the window, her braids swaying as she tilted her head.

"You look like someone just stole your last chocolate bar," Meghna observed.

"Worse," Ishika groaned, flopping onto a dust-covered bench. "I have a math test tomorrow, and I'm going to fail again."

Meghna leaned forward, her elbows resting on the windowsill. "Math isn't scary, Ishika. It's just sneaky—like a puzzle you have to figure out."

Ishika threw up her hands. "I don't want to figure it out! I want to set it on fire."

Meghna sighed dramatically. "Fine. Let's make a deal."

Ishika narrowed her eyes. "What kind of deal?"

"For every math problem you solve correctly, I'll give you a life-changing secret."

Ishika sat up a little. "Secrets about what?"

Meghna smirked. "Secrets about people, about the world. Maybe even about Varun."

Ishika froze.

Varun was the smartest boy in the class, the one whose confidence made teachers nod approvingly. He had a dimpled smile that made Ishika's entire nervous system shut down.

Meghna's smirk deepened. "Oh? Now you're interested?"

Ishika crossed her arms. "This is manipulation."

"This is motivation." Meghna winked. "Come on, Ishika. Let's outsmart math—one problem at a time."

And so, the battle began.

That evening, Ishika sat in her room, determined. She opened her math textbook.

"Okay," she muttered. "Let's do this."

For the first time, she approached math like a puzzle rather than a nightmare.

Problem #1: A train leaves the station at 6:00 a.m…

Meghna's voice echoed in her mind. "Math is just a story with missing pieces. Fill in the gaps."

Ishika focused, solved the problem, and checked her answer. It was correct. A thrill ran through her.

The next day, she ran to the window, breathless. "I did it! I solved five problems!"

Meghna clapped. "I'm impressed. Ready for your reward?"

Ishika grinned. "Tell me something about Varun."

Meghna leaned in, lowering her voice conspiratorially. "He notices you more than you think."

Ishika's stomach flipped. "Liar."

Meghna just smiled. "Solve five more, and I'll prove it."

And just like that, math was not so unbearable anymore.

Ishika had never thought of herself as special. She was neither the girl who won medals nor the one whose name teachers mentioned with pride. She existed in the background—blurry and forgettable—until Meghna said otherwise.

It started on a rainy afternoon.

Ishika trudged into the abandoned wing, her uniform damp and her mood worse. Meghna, as always, was perched by the window, dry and effortlessly unbothered.

"You look like a tragic heroine," Meghna observed, flicking an imaginary speck of dust from her sleeve.

Ishika groaned. "I had to read my English essay in class today."

Meghna brightened. "Oh? And?"

"And everyone stared at me like I'd grown two heads."

Meghna raised an eyebrow. "Was it because it was bad, or because it was too good?"

Ishika hesitated.

The truth was that her teacher had been impressed. There had been an odd silence in the room when she finished reading. Even Varun had turned in his seat.

"But Ishika?" she panicked, trying to downplay it, brushing it off as mere luck.

"Stories are just silly words," she mumbled. "Anyone can write them."

Meghna's expression darkened.

"Wrong."

Ishika blinked. Meghna rarely looked angry.

Leaning closer, Meghna's voice sharpened. "Not everyone can paint pictures with words. Not everyone can trap emotions on a page. You can."

Ishika opened her mouth to respond, but Meghna was not finished.

"Do you know what your problem is?" she continued. "You're afraid of being seen."

Ishika tensed.

"You write," Meghna said, "but you don't let the world read. You speak, but you pull back before anyone can listen. You hide your talent as if it's something to be ashamed of."

Ishika swallowed hard.

Meghna exhaled, shaking her head. Then she did something unexpected.

She pulled out an old notebook from behind the windowpane. Its pages were yellowed, and the cover was scratched.

"What's this?" Ishika asked.

Meghna smiled faintly. "A gift. Write in it—everything - Your thoughts, your stories, your ridiculous daydreams about Varun."

Ishika flushed. "I don't daydream about Varun."

Meghna grinned. "Are you sure?"

Ishika hesitated before taking the notebook. It felt important.

That night, under the dim glow of her bedside lamp, she opened it.

And for the first time, she wrote.

Not for school. Not for grades. Not for anyone else. Just for herself.

She filled the first page with a story about a lonely girl who found a friend in a forgotten place.

When she read it back, she smiled—because, for the first time, she saw herself in her own words.

Ishika's worst nightmare was not ghosts, monsters, or failing a math test.

It was standing before an audience.

Unfortunately, fate—and her teacher—had conspired against her.

"You'll be representing our class in the debate competition," her English teacher announced one morning.

Ishika nearly choked on air.

"But, ma'am—" she began, only to be cut off by a firm look.

"No excuses, Ishika. You have a strong voice when you choose to use it. The competition is in two weeks. Prepare well."

And just like that, doomsday was set.

That afternoon, she rushed to the abandoned wing, her pulse hammering.

Meghna took one look at her and sighed dramatically. "Let me guess—you finally confessed your undying love to Varun, and he ran away?"

Ishika scowled. "Worse. I have to speak in front of people in a debate competition."

Meghna grinned. "Oh, this is going to be fun."

Ishika gaped. "Fun?! I'm going to embarrass myself in front of the entire school!"

Meghna rolled her eyes. "Drama queen. You'll be fine."

"No, I won't! My voice will shake, I'll forget my points, and then I'll probably faint!"

Meghna smirked. "Okay, okay. Since you're one gasp away from a meltdown, let's fix this."

She straightened and tapped the windowpane. "Lesson one: public speaking is all about confidence."

Ishika groaned. "Well, I don't have any."

Meghna wagged a finger. "Ah, but you can pretend you do. Nobody knows what's going on inside your head. Walk in like you own the stage."

Ishika frowned. "That sounds like lying."

Meghna grinned. "Darling, it's called acting. The world's best speakers are just good actors."

Ishika bit her lip. "Okay, what if I forget everything mid-speech?"

Meghna waved a hand. "Then pause. Look thoughtful. Make the audience think it's intentional."

Ishika narrowed her eyes. "Does that work?"

Meghna smirked. "Like a charm. And if all else fails, imagine them in their underwear."

Ishika recoiled. "That's disgusting!"

"Exactly!" Meghna laughed. "You'll be too horrified to be nervous."

Ishika groaned. "You're impossible."

Meghna grinned. "I prefer the term brilliant."

The auditorium was packed. The microphone loomed like an executioner. Ishika's hands trembled as she walked onto the stage.

She could feel hundreds of eyes on her.

Her heart pounded.

Then a voice in her head whispered, *Walk in like you own the stage.*

She lifted her chin, took a breath, and stepped forward.

She stumbled over a word in her opening line. Panic surged—but she stopped, breathed, and pretended to consider her next words.

The audience waited.

She continued, this time stronger.

And then it happened.

Halfway through her argument, Meghna's absurd advice popped into her mind. She imagined the audience in their underwear—and almost burst out laughing.

Instead of fear, she felt amusement.

Her voice steadied, her words flowed, and by the time she finished, applause filled the room.

She had done it.

That evening, Ishika raced to the window.

Meghna was already there, smirking.

Ishika was still breathless with excitement. "I—I won!"

Meghna's smile widened. "Of course you did."

Ishika shook her head in disbelief. "I still can't believe it."

Meghna leaned against the frame. "Believe it, Ishika. You were always meant to shine. You just needed a little push."

For the first time, Ishika believed in herself.

Ishika had three major fears in life:

- Public speaking (which she had miraculously conquered),
- Mathematics (which Meghna was still trying to fix), and
- Making a complete fool of herself in front of Varun.

The problem was that Varun was perfect.

He was not only the smartest boy in class—he was the kind of person who made algebra look effortless and could win debates without breaking a sweat. He was polite, charming, and always had a book in his hand.

Ishika, on the other hand, turned into a stuttering mess whenever he was around.

She sighed heavily as she reached the abandoned wing. Meghna, lounging by the window as usual, instantly sensed that something was wrong.

"Oh dear," Meghna drawled, examining Ishika like a scientist inspecting a failed experiment. "Let me guess—you saw Varun today and forgot how to function?"

Ishika groaned, saying, "It's getting worse. I swear, the moment he talks to me, my brain just shuts down."

Meghna smirked and said, "Classic case of academic crush syndrome—deadly, but curable."

Ishika buried her face in her hands. "It's hopeless."

Meghna clapped her hands together. "Alright, my dear disaster, let's get to work. It's time for your next lesson."

Ishika peeked through her fingers. "Next lesson?"

Meghna grinned. "Yes—welcome to the Science of Attraction."

"First things first," Meghna declared, "You have to stop staring at him like he's some rare species you're trying to catch."

"I do not—" Ishika began.

Before she could finish, Meghna held up a hand. "Sweetheart, you definitely do. You practically follow him with your eyes like you have an inbuilt GPS and he's your destination."

Ishika groaned. "Then what do I do?"

Meghna leaned in, her eyes twinkling. "Simple. Make him notice you instead."

Ishika frowned. "How?"

Meghna smirked. "By doing what you're best at—being brilliant."

The next lesson was called the "Be Unbothered" strategy.

Meghna tapped the windowpane. "Do you know what's irresistible? Confidence. People are drawn to those who own their space."

"I don't have confidence," Ishika muttered.

"Yes, you do," Meghna shot back. "Remember the debate? You walked in like you owned the stage. That's what you need to do—in life, in conversations, and especially around Varun."

Ishika sighed. "So I just pretend to be confident?"

"Exactly," Meghna replied. "Act like you have better things to do than be affected by his existence."

"That sounds fake," Ishika said hesitantly.

"It's a strategy," Meghna countered. "Watch. Tomorrow, instead of panicking, just nod and smile when he talks to you. No weird stammering, no staring—just be cool."

"Easier said than done," Ishika muttered.

"Trust me," Meghna said with a wink. "It works."

The next lesson was called the "Subtle Interest" test.

The following day, Ishika put Meghna's advice to the test. During lunch, she sat at her desk, pretending to be completely absorbed in her book.

At that moment, Varun walked past. He slowed down—and then, to Ishika's utter shock, he stopped.

"Hey, Ishika," he said.

Her heart nearly exploded, but she remembered Meghna's words. Be cool.

She looked up slowly, smiled, and nodded. "Hey, Varun."

Then she went back to reading.

There was a brief silence.

For a second, panic crept in. Had she overdone it? Had she just ignored him?

But then Varun chuckled and asked, "What are you reading?"

Ishika glanced up again, forcing herself to breathe normally. She replied, "A mystery novel."

His eyes lit up. "Nice! I love mysteries. Agatha Christie?"

Ishika smiled and said, "Sherlock Holmes, actually."

Varun grinned and said, "Oh, I have thoughts on Sherlock. Mind if I sit?"

Ishika blinked. *Did he just ask to sit with me?*

Struggling to keep her voice steady, she replied, "Sure."

As Varun pulled up a chair, Ishika screamed internally. Somewhere, she was certain Meghna was smirking triumphantly.

The next lesson: the law of attraction.

That evening, Ishika rushed to the window, beaming. Meghna was already there, looking smug.

"It worked!" Ishika gushed. "He talked to me—he even sat with me at lunch!"

Meghna inspected her nails. "Ah, the wonders of my genius."

Ishika laughed. "You should have seen his face when I didn't stutter like an idiot."

"I told you," Meghna said with a smirk. "Confidence is magnetic."

Ishika nodded, still giddy. Then a thought struck her.

"Meghna?"

"Hmm?"

"How do you know all this?"

Meghna's smirk froze.

For a split second, her expression shifted—something almost melancholic flickered in her eyes. But just as quickly, she masked it with a grin.

"Sweetheart, I know a lot of things."

Ishika stared at her.

"Some questions," Meghna had once said, "are better left unanswered." Ishika decided not to press further.

Ishika had never imagined a world without Meghna.

For months, their stolen lunchtime meetings had been the highlight of her day. The girl behind the window had been her secret, her mentor, her anchor.

So, on the last day of school after her Class 12 board exams, Ishika ran down the familiar, dust-laden corridor, eager to tell Meghna everything.

She had aced her exams. She had finally mastered algebra and calculus. And most importantly, Varun had asked for her number.

Breathless with excitement, she reached the forgotten window.

But Meghna was not there.

Ishika frowned. She pressed her face against the cold glass, scanning the empty space beyond.

"Meghna?" she called softly.

There was Silence.

A strange unease slithered down her spine. Meghna had never missed a meeting. Even on the days Ishika was sick, Meghna had been there—waiting, teasing, always knowing exactly what to say.

"Maybe she's late," Ishika reasoned, though Meghna had never been late before.

She waited and waited, but Meghna never came.

By the end of the school day, worry gnawed at her insides. The rational part of her mind told her she was overreacting.

The irrational part of her mind whispered something she did not want to admit—something felt wrong.

Desperate, she began searching.

She asked around, keeping her voice carefully casual.

"Hey, do you know a girl named Meghna?"

Every answer was the same:

"Meghna who?"

"Never heard of her."

"Are you sure she goes to our school?"

The panic began as a slow trickle, and then grew into a flood.

How could no one know her? Meghna had worn their school uniform. She had spoken about teachers, students, and homework. She had to be real.

That evening, Ishika found herself back at the window.

For the first time, the abandoned wing felt truly desolate.

She ran her fingers over the familiar cracks in the wooden frame, as if hoping they would reveal a hidden message.

"Where did you go, Meghna?"

Her chest ached. The silence was unbearable.

Then her eyes fell on something small and out of place.

A tiny wooden box sat on the windowsill, coated in dust, along with the same old notebook Meghna had given her to write stories and poems—as if it had been waiting for her all along. The wooden box resembled the gift her mother had once given her for Christmas. How had Meghna found one just like it? And how had the notebook come to be there?

She turned the pages slowly. The poems inside were raw and luminous, words strung together like veins of memory. They spoke of fear, of courage, of a girl learning to see herself.

But what startled her most were not the verses—it was the handwriting.

It was hers, every curve, every tilt, and every hesitant loop. The poems felt not only written for her, but written by her.

She sat there for a long while, the notebook open on her lap, her fingers trembling over the ink that looked both foreign and familiar.

"You found me where you began."

She looked up. The window glowed faintly in the fading light. Her reflection shimmered, and then blurred into something that almost resembled a smile.

Meghna, she realised, had never wanted to be found. She wanted to remain—like these words—hidden between lines, breathing through pages.

And as Ishika closed the notebook, a thought brushed past her like a breeze: perhaps Meghna had never disappeared at all.

Perhaps she had only become the story.

She read the last line of the notebook again: *"The greatest journey you'll ever take is the one in which you find your own reflection in the mirror of your soul."*

2

Miss Ratna's Magical Bag

Miss Ratna's bag was ancient. Its once-bright fabric had faded with time, and the stitches were stretched thin, like secrets barely holding together. It hung from her shoulder like a relic from another era, unremarkable to the untrained eye. But to the children of Vidya Niketan School, that bag was legendary.

They swore it was magical.

How else could one explain how the weakest students of Class VI-A transformed so dramatically?

Ganesh, who once stuttered so badly that he could barely introduce himself, sang a flawless Lata Mangeshkar melody on Independence Day, leaving even the stern principal dabbing his eyes with a handkerchief.

Shrini, who had once believed algebra was a sadistic prank invented by aliens, now walked into math class as if it were her kingdom, scoring a perfect hundred on her latest test.

The corridors buzzed with whispers.

"It's the chits," the students said. "She pulls out a chit… and boom—magic happens."

But it had not always been this way.

Miss Ratna had a gift—not of potions or spells, but of perception. She noticed the subtle tremble in a child's voice, the slump of disappointment in their shoulders, and the silence of those who had stopped trying.

She never raised her voice; she did not need to. Her silence was soothing, her presence steadying.

She had seen Shrini's struggle firsthand—the way the girl clenched her pencil until her knuckles whitened, staring at her math notebook as if it might bite. When called upon, Shrini would fumble, mumble, and eventually pretend to search for a lost pen, her head bowed in humiliation.

One rainy afternoon, with the classroom windows blurred by monsoon mist, Miss Ratna called Shrini to the front.

"Shrini," she said gently, "today we're going to try something a little magical."

From her mysterious bag, she pulled out a handful of matchsticks.

The class giggled. "Magic with matchsticks?" someone whispered.

Undeterred, Miss Ratna laid them on Shrini's desk and began forming patterns. "Look," she said. "Math isn't just numbers. It is puzzles, patterns, pictures."

She turned 'x + x + x' into '3x' with three swift arrangements. "This is all it is—a different way of seeing."

Something shifted in Shrini's eyes.

Day by day, Miss Ratna transformed formulas into games, equations into art, and fear into fascination. Matchsticks became fractions, stories turned into word problems, and algebra lost its sting.

Then came the test results.

Shrini stared at the bold 100/100 in disbelief. Her hands trembled as she clutched her answer sheet and rushed to Miss Ratna.

"Ma'am… I—I did it!"

Miss Ratna smiled, her voice barely above a whisper.

"You always could, Shrini. You just hadn't believed it yet."

She worked her quiet magic on others, too.

Arun's energy bounced off the walls; most teachers saw him as a disruption. Mrs Gupta, the strictest teacher in the school, often muttered that some students were "beyond saving."

One morning, Miss Ratna pulled a chit from her bag and read aloud: "Arun will be the school's chess champion."

The class burst into laughter: *Chess?* He could barely sit still for five minutes.

Miss Ratna handed him the chit. It was blank.

He looked up, puzzled. "Ma'am, it's empty."

She smiled. "Then perhaps you already know what to do."

And that was enough.

Out of curiosity—or perhaps to prove her wrong—Arun began playing chess. His first few games ended in quick, humbling defeats. But something about the quiet battle of strategy intrigued him. Over time, his restless energy found direction, turning into sharp, tactical thinking.

Months later, he stood holding a glinting trophy—the inter-school chess championship.

"I don't know what's crazier," he said, half-laughing, half-amazed. "That I'm winning, or that I love it."

Maya was a quiet girl who loved colours but guarded her art as if it were a secret. Years ago, she had entered a school art competition with a bold, abstract sketch while others drew predictable sunsets and smiling suns. Her piece stood out—but not in the way she had hoped. The judges looked puzzled, her classmates snickered, and she never painted in public again.

One morning, Miss Ratna called her name.

"Maya will paint the school's annual mural."

Maya froze. Her stomach dropped. Paint the mural?

Miss Ratna handed her a chit—another blank one.

"There's nothing written," Maya whispered.

"Exactly," Miss Ratna replied, "Because the vision is already inside you."

That night, Maya painted. At first, she was hesitant, but later she grew her confidence. Her brush stopped apologizing and began to move freely. The mural she created was unlike anything the school had seen—bold, chaotic, and beautiful.

When it was unveiled, even the principal—who narrowly avoided being splattered—stood speechless.

"Okay," Maya admitted with a shy smile, "maybe she is magic."

But not everyone was convinced.

Mrs Gupta, the sternest teacher at Vidya Niketan, watched Miss Ratna with growing suspicion. Magic? Nonsense. Education, in her view, was built on discipline, hard work, and red ink.

And that bag—it had to be hiding something. Cheat sheets? Hypnosis guides? Secret psychology tricks?

One afternoon, when Miss Ratna was called away to the principal's office, Mrs Gupta slipped into the classroom and grabbed the bag. Her hands trembled as she turned it upside down.

Dozens of chits floated down like autumn leaves.

She picked one up. It was blank. She picked up another. It was also blank. All the chits were completely empty.

The door creaked.

She turned around.

Miss Ratna stood in the doorway, arms crossed, calm but amused.

"Looking for something, Mrs Gupta?"

Flustered, Mrs Gupta held up a chit. "They're all blank!"

Miss Ratna stepped forward, picked up a chit, and with a hint of theatrical flair, read aloud:

"Mrs Gupta will now understand that belief is the most powerful magic of all."

Mrs Gupta blinked. Something in her expression softened.

She looked around the classroom—Shrini's test proudly pinned on the wall, Arun's trophy gleaming on the shelf, Maya's mural blazing across the corridor. The evidence was undeniable.

It was never about tricks.

It was about trust—about unlocking potential with a quiet whisper of belief.

Miss Ratna smiled gently. "The magic was never in the bag, Mrs Gupta. It was in them. I only reminded them of what they had forgotten—or never knew."

Outside, the bell rang. Children poured into the hallways, their laughter ringing like a song.

Shrini walked tall, no longer shrinking from the world.

Arun traced imaginary chess moves in the air.

Maya stood proudly beside her mural, colours still bright on her fingers.

Miss Ratna gathered her blank chits, slung the old bag over her shoulder, and walked toward the staffroom. At the doorway, she paused.

"Sometimes," she said softly, "all a child needs is someone who believes in them before they believe in themselves."

Then she walked away, her bag rustling with invisible dreams, her quiet magic planted in every heart she had touched.

3

Letters from the Sky

The air in Pondicherry in mid-August carried the scent of salt and rain-washed stone, as though the city had been cleansed by the monsoon and left to dry under muted sunlight. Cobblestones still gleamed with dampness, and balconies spilt bougainvillaea in sudden bursts of pink, as if beauty refused to hide even in a season of grief.

Vedant walked these streets differently now. His feet dragged, his shoulders slumped. He was only seven, yet his father's death in June had burdened him with years beyond his age. His father had been the kind of man whose laughter filled rooms, who lifted his son high enough to make him believe he could touch the sky. Then, one ordinary evening, his heart had simply stopped. The absence he left behind was not loud, but constant—like a ceiling fan still whirring in a dark, empty room.

At home, grief clung to the walls. His mother moved mechanically, her bangles silent. The faint scent of vetiver and incense lingered, but the warmth had faded. Vedant had learned how silence could bruise.

What he held onto instead were memories—one in particular. Every Independence Day, Appa would wake him before dawn, and together they would walk to Gandhi Thidal Beach. There, they flew Shanku, a shark-shaped kite stitched from saree scraps and tied with strong fishing nylon.

"India is freedom," Appa would say, his eyes glinting as the kite soared. "And freedom belongs to everyone. Flying Shanku is our salute to the sky."

This year, Vedant walked to the beach alone.

The sand was wet, the waves restless, and the morning wind unforgiving. He raised Shanku anyway, his small hands clumsy on the reel. For a moment, the kite danced as it always had. Then a sudden tug snapped the string, and Shanku shot upward, disappearing into the grey sky like a spirit set free.

Vedant stood barefoot, the frayed thread hanging uselessly, tears streaking his cheeks.

That was when Mr Krishnamurthy noticed him.

A retired art teacher, he spent his mornings sketching by the shore. His hair resembled sea foam, and his fingers were faintly stained with charcoal. Over the years, he had quietly watched Vedant and his father fly their kite, their joy as visible as the kite itself. Now, he saw the boy standing alone, diminished by grief.

Krishnamurthy sat beside him without speaking. The sea filled the silence. Finally, in a voice as thin as worn paper, he said, "Lost him, didn't you?"

Vedant nodded, still staring at the clouds.

The old man's eyes softened. He carried his own losses, though the boy could not yet understand. Years ago, he had lost his only son to a fever that medicine could not cure. His son had been restless, always dreaming of travelling to distant places—temples, deserts, mountains—drawn from the pages of his books. After his death, Krishnamurthy had travelled alone, sketchbook in hand, as though completing his son's unfinished journeys.

Now, looking at Vedant, something stirred within him. He felt compelled to pass on what he once wished he could give his own child.

"Kites that are loved don't vanish," he said gently. "They go exploring."

Vedant frowned, uncertain.

"Perhaps Shanku will write to you," Krishnamurthy added softly. "Come tomorrow. He might send a letter."

The next evening, under a sky washed in soft orange light, Krishnamurthy handed Vedant a folded note sealed with a yellow fish sticker. The paper carried a faint scent of paint and lemongrass oil.

Vedant opened it with trembling fingers.

From the Sky Desk of Shanku the Shark-Kite

Vedant,

I'm sorry I flew away. The wind carried me to Mahabalipuram. I saw the stone chariots Appa once told us about, carved from single rocks. The sea there roars like drums. I remembered how Appa guided your hand the first time we flew. I miss him too.

I'll write again soon. I'm on a journey.

—Shanku

Vedant pressed the letter to his chest. For the first time since June, he smiled.

In the weeks that followed, a quiet correspondence unfolded—like a secret conversation with the sky. Each Sunday brought a new letter, sometimes decorated with charcoal sketches, sometimes with a pressed flower tucked inside.

From Gujarat:

The Rann looks like salt but feels like secrets. A boy here dances garba better than he walks. Colours brighter than peacocks, food spicier than secrets Appa never told.

Vedant remembered how his father once lifted him on his shoulders during Navratri at the ashram, both of them clapping badly out of rhythm. He laughed softly, almost embarrassed by the memory, but grateful.

From Kashmir:

Snow, Vedant! White as idlis but cold enough to sting. I glided above Dal Lake, where shikaras drift like dreams. The mountains whispered old prayers. Missing Appa is part of the journey, isn't it?

Vedant touched the page, imagining the sting of snow on cheeks. He whispered to himself, *Yes, Appa is everywhere.*

From Odisha:

Drums thundered in Puri. Even the gods travel here, pulled on chariots. I saw the Konark wheel that tells time, not straight but circling, like memory.

Vedant traced the sketch of a wheel. For days, he thought about time, how Appa's laughter circled back each night in dreams.

From Sikkim:

Prayer flags are like cousins to me. A monk gave me silence, the kind that fills you. Flying is not always rushing forward. Sometimes, flying is learning to stay still in the wind.

Vedant held the letter to his ear as though silence itself might spill from it.

From the Thar Desert:

A camel nearly ate me! Rajasthan is a painting you can walk inside – Forts singing, colours arguing, winds carrying old tales. A puppeteer told me, "Stories are how we remember those who left." So I danced harder, for Appa.

Vedant began telling these stories to his mother at night. Slowly, she began to listen, and her silences softened.

Through it all, Vedant never questioned the magic. It was easier to believe that his kite had found a voice.

Then one Sunday, no letter arrived.

Instead, Krishnamurthy came with a cloth-wrapped bundle. Inside was a handcrafted wind chime shaped like a shark kite. Its wooden fins were painted with symbols—a chariot, a lotus, a wheel, a prayer flag, a camel, and a desert sun.

Vedant frowned. "But this isn't Shanku."

The old man handed him one final note.

Vedant,

I have flown through sunshine and snowfall, met laughter and longing, danced to drums and prayed with the wind. I am no longer stitched cloth. I am memory carved into wood. I will not fly again, but I will sing by your window whenever the wind remembers.

Just like Appa, I will always be near, even if you cannot see me.

—Shanku

That night, Vedant hung the chime by his window. When the breeze stirred, its sound was neither wood nor metal—it was something softer, something freer.

Time moved forward, as it always does, carrying with it echoes and scents of what had been.

Vedant grew into a young man. His room in Pondicherry was filled with books, maps, and notebooks brimming with sketches and stories. The chime still sang by his window.

He went on to study cultural anthropology. His professors often marvelled at the way he connected landscapes with stories, rituals with memory. His knowledge came not just from books, but from something deeper—from letters carried by the wind.

One winter, while sorting through an old trunk his mother had kept, Vedant discovered a bundle of charcoal sketches, drafts of letters, and carefully preserved notes about temples, deserts, and distant places.

That was when he understood that there had never been a magical kite—only a man who had once lost a son, and who chose to heal a grieving child with stories.

It was not a trick. It was love, disguised as magic.

Years later, Vedant published a book titled *Winds of Wonder: Letters from Shanku the Kite*. It was more than a travelogue—it was a memoir, a tribute, a quiet love letter to both Appa and Mr Krishnamurthy.

At a literature festival, during a reading session, a young girl raised her hand and asked, "Was Shanku real?"

Vedant paused, listening to the wind rustling through nearby trees, remembering the chime of his childhood.

"He was real in the only way that matters," Vedant said softly. "He was my father's love, my country's stories, and one old man's way of helping me find the sky again."

Somewhere beyond the hall, the wind stirred—and a chime began to sing.

4

The Happiness Cactus

"The cactus, long silent and still, felt the change in the air. With a pulse of joy, it bloomed for the first time, sensing happiness deeper than the heart itself."

Rashmi had discovered the cactus in a quaint nursery tucked into the heart of Cairo's old market. She had not intended to buy a plant, yet something about it drew her in—its quiet presence, its spiny resilience. The old shopkeeper smiled knowingly as he wrapped the pot.

"This one brings joy where it is needed most," he said, his voice carrying the weight of an ancient promise.

Back home, Rashmi wasted no time visiting Vrinda and Sameer, her favourite couple, carrying the cactus as a housewarming gift. She had missed their party because of her trip.

"Who brings a cactus as a gift?" Vrinda scoffed, eyeing the prickly plant with open dismay. "And who said it would flower? I see no sign of it. You and your unusual taste, Rashmi—just like that saree you gave me for my wedding. Who wears one with Buddha's teachings handwritten on it?"

Sameer, Vrinda's husband, gave her a subtle look—a silent signal to soften her words. Rashmi, however, remained unfazed. She and Vrinda had always been brutally honest with each other; their friendship thrived on their differences. Vrinda was practical and no-nonsense, while Rashmi saw the world through a lens of mystery and wonder.

"How was Egypt?" Vrinda asked, changing the subject.

"Magical," Rashmi replied, her eyes lighting up. "There's something powerful about that place. I felt drawn to it in a way I can't explain. In fact, I've enrolled in a course on Egyptian studies at JNU. I'm leaving for Delhi next week."

Vrinda nodded, barely glancing at the cactus as she placed it on the balcony. It sat there quietly, absorbing light, air, and the unspoken dreams that filled their home.

Yet inside the house, happiness was slipping through the cracks.

Seven years had passed in whispered prayers and doctor visits that ended in quiet disappointment. Vrinda still remembered the hope in Sameer's eyes during their first year together—choosing baby names, imagining a nursery. Over time, those dreams faded into unanswered questions and hollow reassurances.

The weight of it all lay between them. It showed in the way Sameer's voice lost its brightness when someone asked, "Any good news?" It lingered in the way Vrinda avoided family gatherings, and in the sharp words they sometimes exchanged—words they regretted but never took back.

One evening, after another disheartening doctor's visit, the tension finally broke.

"This isn't fair," Vrinda whispered, staring at the floor. "I've done everything—the diets, the treatments, the medicines. Why is this happening to us?"

Sameer sat beside her in silence.

"Say something," she snapped. "Aren't you frustrated? Or have you just given up?"

His jaw tightened. "What do you want me to say, Vrinda? That I cry in the shower sometimes? That I feel useless every time I see you break down? That I hate watching you suffer and not being able to fix it?"

She turned away, biting her lip. They were not fighting each other; they were fighting the same pain. Yet some nights, it felt as though the pain was winning.

That night, unable to sleep, Vrinda stepped onto the balcony. The cactus stood there, its spiny arms reaching toward the sky. She touched it absentmindedly, its rough texture grounding her thoughts.

She let out a breath she had not realised she was holding.

Something about the plant soothed her, as though it absorbed the words she could not say. Gradually, she began spending more time outside—watching the sunrise, whispering her thoughts into the cool night air.

"I feel like you understand," she murmured one evening, tracing the rim of its pot. "You don't ask questions. You don't make me feel broken. You just exist."

One night, Sameer found her gently watering the cactus.

"Since when did you become a plant lover?" he teased, leaning against the railing.

Vrinda shrugged, smiling softly. "It listens. It doesn't judge. It feels like it absorbs all my worries."

Sameer chuckled, and then hesitated before stepping closer. "Maybe I should start talking to it, too. Work's been tough. The merger—and the possible downsizing—have been taking a toll on me."

Little by little, the cactus became their silent companion.

Sameer, who once escaped his stress through late-night drives, now found himself on the balcony, fingers tracing the cactus's rough surface. He would sit there after exhausting days, speaking softly about difficult meetings, family pressures, and his guilt over not being able to ease Vrinda's pain.

Strangely, with every word he released, he felt lighter—as if the cactus listened without judgment, quietly absorbing it all.

Gradually, the heaviness in their home began to lift. The arguments lessened, replaced by long conversations under the stars. Laughter, hesitant at first, slowly returned.

Then, one morning, Vrinda gasped.

A single white flower had bloomed on the cactus.

She called Sameer, her voice trembling with wonder. "Look! It's blooming! You said it wouldn't—but it has!"

Startled by her excitement, Sameer rushed over. The delicate flower, stark against the cactus's thorny body, felt nothing short of miraculous.

"After all this time," Vrinda whispered, touching the petals as though they might vanish.

"It's like..." Sameer began, and then paused.

"A sign?" Vrinda finished, her eyes shining.

That night, a soft breeze moved through their home, carrying with it an unspoken sense of change—something neither of them could fully name.

And as if the universe had been waiting for that moment, another miracle followed.

That very month, Vrinda discovered she was expecting.

Tears filled her eyes as she held Sameer's hand. The happiness they had longed for had finally arrived, as though carried on the whisper of an ancient blessing, wrapped in the silent strength of a cactus.

Months later, when Rashmi visited again, Vrinda greeted her with a radiant smile, one hand resting on her growing belly.

"You were right," she said, gently touching the now-flourishing cactus. "Some things really do bring joy where it's needed most."

Rashmi smiled, her gaze lingering on the plant. "Or perhaps," she said softly, "joy was always within you. The cactus only reminded you how to bloom again."

As the wind whispered across the balcony, the cactus stood tall—a silent witness to resilience, love, and the quiet miracles that unfold when hope refuses to wither.

5

The Birth of a Storyteller

The Golden Book Café hummed with the soft murmur of readers, their voices rising and falling like waves against walls lined with bookshelves. At the centre sat Ruchi Bhatiya, her golden Parker pen gleaming as though it had absorbed the glow of every story she had ever written. When she signed her name, the ink seemed to shimmer faintly, as if it carried more than mere letters—perhaps fragments of her soul.

One by one, readers stepped forward, books pressed to their chests like talismans. The air was thick with anticipation, as though each autograph was not just a signature, but an initiation into her secret world.

When the last book closed, a voice broke through the hush.

"Where did it all begin?"

The question startled Ruchi more than she expected. She looked up to see a man with sharp eyes, a press badge glinting under the lights: Ritesh Sharma from Global Media Ltd. Unlike the others, he had not come for an autograph. His gaze was not that of a fan, but of someone intent on unlocking hidden doors.

"I've read your novels," he said. "The diary always appears. The lonely protagonist always whispers to it when the world falls silent. Even your most fantastical stories carry that thread. Tell me, Ms Ruchi—are you confessing through your fiction? Is the diary yours?"

The room fell silent. Even the coffee machine seemed to pause.

Ruchi smiled, though something fragile flickered within it. She lifted the microphone.

"It began," she said, "the day I realised words could live, even when no one listened."

Her eyes softened as memory drew her back.

"As a child, I came home every evening brimming with stories. 'You know what happened today…' was my ritual. At first, my parents listened kindly, but soon they would drift off to sleep; my sister would roll her eyes until they disappeared behind her fingers. Still, I spoke—because the telling mattered more than being heard.

"But one afternoon, I came home with a story that truly mattered. Something at school had hurt me. I rehearsed every detail on the bus, shaping it into the perfect telling. Yet when I arrived, they were already lying down, eyes closed, as if they had rehearsed too. It was the first time I felt a story die on my tongue."

A quiet stillness settled over the café.

"I was nine—too young to understand their exhaustion, yet old enough to feel hurt and betrayed. That's when I noticed my father's unused diary on his desk, its blank pages glowing faintly in the late afternoon light. I opened it, and it seemed to wait for me. So I wrote my story there. And to my surprise, the diary listened. It did not sigh, or sleep, or turn away. It held every word.

"The next day, I wrote again and then again. At first, I wrote only what was real. But soon… the diary began to whisper back."

Her voice dropped to a hush.

"One evening, I wrote about something strange. I described how our neighbourhood would flood after a sudden rain, how a red umbrella would drift down the street, and how an old man I had never met would knock on our door for shelter. It was only imagination—or so I believed. But the very next week, it happened. Every detail. The umbrella, the knock, the trembling voice asking for water. It was as though my diary had decided to test its own power."

The audience shifted uneasily—some leaning forward, others drawn in as if caught in an invisible web.

"That was when I realised," she continued, "my words don't just live. Sometimes... they breathe."

A collective breath passed through the room, a mixture of awe and disbelief.

Ritesh leaned forward. "So, are you saying your fiction bleeds into reality?"

Ruchi tilted her head, her pen catching the light. "Or perhaps reality bleeds into my fiction. Perhaps they conspire together."

A nervous ripple of laughter moved through the audience.

Then, with a mischievous glint in her eyes, she added, "In fact, I wrote this entire evening in my diary. I even wrote about how the man with a press badge would question me—and how all of you would gasp and whisper at this very moment."

The audience froze, exchanging uncertain glances. A wave of gasps followed—exactly as she had described.

Ruchi flipped a page of her diary theatrically and smiled. "And here," she said, tapping it lightly, "I wrote that when I read this aloud, you would burst into laughter."

The crowd hesitated, suspended between doubt and expectation.

Ruchi leaned closer to the microphone, lowering her voice. "And just to be certain, I also wrote that the gentleman in the third row, wearing a striped shirt, would laugh so hard that his coffee would spill onto his trousers."

Every head turned.

The man blinked, clutching his paper cup, suddenly self-conscious. For a moment, silence held.

Then the café erupted into laughter—louder than the sputtering coffee machine behind the counter. The man laughed too, shaking his head as he carefully placed his cup on the floor.

Ruchi closed her diary with a soft snap, her smile playful. "Well," she said, "it seems the diary was right again. And don't worry, sir—on the next page, it promises you a free refill."

The room burst into applause, laughter, and cheers. The earlier tension dissolved into warmth and delight. Yet somewhere, beneath the laughter, a quiet question lingered in every mind—

Had she really written it all?

On the table, the golden pen glimmered faintly, as if it were laughing, too, silently witnessing the spell of the storyteller.

6

Teacher on Wheels

Among the millions of stars, some shine quietly, unnoticed. One such star was Raghunath Mishra. His light was gentle, yet it reached places where hope itself had faded.

For decades, Raghunath taught at Gandhi Public School in Rajkot, a modest institution on the outskirts of the bustling city. From his classroom window, he often watched children wandering through the nearby slum lanes—barefoot, dust clinging to their ankles, their eyes burdened with struggles far beyond their years. By day, he taught the French Revolution, quadratic equations, and Shakespeare. By night, he sat in the dim glow of his study, troubled by a single question: what use is knowledge if it never reaches those who need it most?

The school had its rules, and the system its boundaries.

"They are not on the rolls," the authorities would say whenever he asked if slum children could attend his classes, even occasionally. Year after year, he continued teaching—dutiful, yet restless. His lessons ended at the blackboard, but his conscience kept writing questions on the walls of his heart.

When retirement came, it did not feel like an ending, but a release.

He sold his small patch of land and a few family heirlooms, and with the money bought a rusted caravan whose wheels groaned like tired bones. Neighbours whispered and mocked, "The old man has lost his mind." But he worked quietly, transforming the broken vehicle into a moving sanctuary. He built shelves for books, painted a blackboard by hand, arranged benches salvaged from scrap, and set aside a corner for slates and pencils. When it was ready, he placed his hand on the door and named it *Gyaan Rath*—the Chariot of Knowledge.

At first, he worked alone. Gradually, donations began to arrive, helping him acquire charts and textbooks. A solar panel was installed to withstand the harsh Rajkot summers, generating enough power to run lights and a fan inside the van. What began as one man's dream soon grew into something extraordinary.

Every morning, the Rath made its way through the slum lanes. Children ran behind it, their laughter echoing against corrugated roofs like temple bells. Beneath a banyan tree, the caravan would unfold into a classroom.

Here, Raghunath was no longer a retired teacher—he was a man reborn. Algebra became stories of mango sellers, history turned into puppet shows, and English came alive through scenes from *The Jungle Book*. Once, noticing Ayesha from the nearby slum struggling to read, he told her the story of a princess who could not read and was deceived by everyone, until she discovered the power of letters and ruled her land with wisdom. The following week, Ayesha read an entire page aloud. That day, Raghunath turned to the blackboard, hiding tears he could not hold back.

There was Manu, who polished shoes at the railway station and often missed class. One afternoon, Raghunath found him, offered him a sandwich, and asked him to solve a math problem in return. Manu came back the next day, and the next, until he never missed a class again. Years later, he would become a mathematics teacher himself, carrying forward his mentor's legacy.

Raghunath understood that hunger was as formidable an enemy as ignorance. Many mornings, he brought tiffins filled with khichdi, bananas, and parathas. His classroom had no walls, yet it protected dignity. It had no uniforms, yet discipline flourished through care. There were no certificates, yet every child carried lessons etched deep within.

Slowly, the slum began to change. Girls who once stayed home to care for siblings began to dream of becoming doctors. Boys who had never held a pencil started winning scholarships. The *Gyaan Rath* became more than a vehicle—it became a quiet revolution.

Word spread. Local journalists came, followed by national media. Headlines spoke of a "Teacher on Wheels" shaping hundreds of futures. Fame brushed past him, but he remained unchanged. "I only did what I was meant to do," he would say, dressed in his simple, neatly starched kurta, his worn leather-bound lesson planner still tucked under his arm.

Government support later enabled his students to appear for board examinations through open schooling. Volunteers joined him, many of them his former students. Yet he continued to live simply, finding joy only in the brightening eyes of children who now dared to dream.

But time, like chalk on a board, wears away.

One dusky evening, as the horizon glowed with fading light, Raghunath sat inside the Rath, his shawl wrapped tightly around him. Through the open door, he watched the children playing, their laughter carrying promises of a better tomorrow. A deep, quiet peace settled over him.

The next morning, when the caravan reached its usual spot, the children waited. Minutes passed. Silence grew. When they finally looked inside, they found him seated upright, eyes closed, a faint smile on his lips. The lamp had gone out—but only after lighting a thousand others.

Rajkot mourned.

Thousands gathered at his funeral—students, parents, strangers—each carrying a memory, a lesson, a fragment of his kindness. The *Gyaan Rath* was preserved, its journey continuing under the guidance of his students. In every lane it entered, it carried not just books, but his spirit.

Inside the caravan, a small plaque was placed: *"To the teacher who gave us dreams, dignity, and direction. Your lessons will roll on, forever."*

Raghunath Mishra left behind no medals, no grand titles, no monuments of stone. What he left was far greater—lives transformed, futures rewritten, and dignity restored.

Raghunath Mishra did not merely teach. He created worlds, one child at a time.

7

The Dream Job

Recollecting a peculiar dream is never easy, especially when only fragments linger after waking. Yet what made Uncle Satish's dreams so captivating was their resemblance to a treasure hunt.

Uncle Satish was a man of many eccentricities. Tall and lanky, with a mop of unruly hair, he carried an air of mystery about him. His sharp, inquisitive eyes seemed always to be searching for something beyond the ordinary. He had a gift for storytelling, weaving tales that could captivate any audience—especially his nephews, Ritesh and Ravi. Despite his charm, he remained unemployed, not for lack of qualifications, but because he was too lazy to put his knowledge to use. His master's degree in Chemistry lay idle, and the vast estate he had inherited remained uncultivated.

His days were spent reading, chatting, playing with his nephews, and indulging his unusual talent for dreaming. He would slip into a peculiar state: his pulse quickened, his eyes twitched, and he muttered cryptic words. These words often turned out to be clues. At times, when pieced together, they led to remarkable discoveries; at others, he solved puzzles or mathematical problems in his dreams. "The structure of benzene was discovered in a dream," he would often assert, emphasising the importance of his visions.

Most of his dream clues proved accurate, which was credible enough to trust him. His nephews, Ritesh and Ravi, frequently found themselves at the centre of these adventures. Ritesh, the elder at ten, was curious and cautious, always thinking two steps ahead with a keen eye for detail. Ravi, on the other hand, was a spirited seven-year-old, full of boundless energy and infectious enthusiasm. Together, they formed the perfect team, balancing caution with excitement.

The treasures they discovered were far from trivial. Two months earlier, they had unearthed an ancient geometry box in their grandmother's attic. Uncle Satish claimed it dated back to the British era and insisted it was worth its weight in gold. For the boys, the story was easy to believe, especially since the box contained instruments unlike anything they had seen before. Having encountered similar objects in comic books, they trusted his tales completely.

Their grandmother, a kind-hearted woman with a passion for knitting, was always amused by their escapades. She often joined in their excitement, sharing stories from her own childhood. Despite Uncle Satish's peculiarities, she had a soft spot for him and believed in his dreams as much as the boys did.

On another occasion, guided by his dream clues, they discovered an old umbrella in the basement of their Uncle Nishant's farmhouse. Uncle Satish claimed it had originated in Arabia a century ago. "An umbrella in Arabia?" their grandfather scoffed. A retired schoolteacher with a practical outlook, he was often sceptical of Satish's claims. "When did it ever rain there to warrant such an umbrella?" he questioned. But Ritesh and Ravi remained convinced, mesmerised by their uncle's dream-inspired discoveries.

One day, Uncle Satish asked the boys for a head and leg massage to ease himself into his semi-sleep state—the moment when his magic usually occurred. As always, Ritesh and Ravi obliged. Soon, Uncle Satish drifted off, muttering a few words.

"My old farm... rock... tree... pot buried... seeds..." he murmured before falling into a deep sleep. Apart from his usual rapid pulse and twitching, he appeared calm and peaceful.

This time, however, something was different. He had fallen asleep before finishing his clues, leaving the message incomplete.

Determined not to let the mystery slip away, Ritesh and Ravi exchanged excited glances. Grabbing a flashlight and a small spade, they quietly slipped out and made their way to the old farm.

The moon cast eerie shadows along their path. As they approached the farm, Ritesh recalled the words: "rock... tree... pot buried... seeds." They began searching near an ancient, gnarled tree that stood alone in the field.

"Look, Ritesh! There's a large rock next to the tree," whispered Ravi.

They started digging beside the rock, their hearts pounding with anticipation. After what felt like hours, the spade struck something hard.

Ravi's eyes widened as they uncovered a small, rusted pot. With trembling hands, Ritesh lifted the lid, revealing a collection of old seeds.

"We found it!" Ravi exclaimed, unable to contain his excitement.

Their discovery felt extraordinary. Once again, Uncle Satish's dream had led them to a hidden treasure. They hurried back home, eager to share the news, certain that this was only the beginning of many more adventures.

Their grandfather examined the pot and deciphered the mystery. Inside was a message inscribed on a palm leaf: "These are magical seeds. If planted and well cared for, they will yield magical fruits. They are worth their weight in gold."

Uncle Satish was astonished that his dream had been so precise. Ritesh and Ravi could hardly wait to sow the seeds. But planting them meant preparing the long-barren land—land that had been neglected for years by Uncle Satish himself.

News spread through the village like wildfire. The next day, people gathered to inspect the seeds. No one had ever seen anything quite like them. The excitement in the air stirred something within Uncle Satish, inspiring him to prepare the land and take up farming for the first time. Ritesh and Ravi encouraged him, promising to stand by him and remind him of this dream come true, just like all the others.

Their grandfather was the happiest of all. With a mischievous smile, he remarked, "If there could be steel umbrellas in Arabia a hundred years ago, then even this barren land can bear fruit today. One only needs to work hard."

With a twinkle in his eye, he took a few seeds and tossed them toward the field. "Let the magic begin," cheered the villagers.

From that day on, Uncle Satish became a farmer—guided, at last, by his own dream.

SECTION II

Love, Loss & Longing

8

The Sunflower in His Bow

"This Sunday, I'm going to bake an apple pie!" Arya announced, her eyes sparkling like dew in the early sunlight. "But I'll need your help plucking apples from Dhruva's orchard. I want a whole basketful."

Arjun looked up from the arrow shaft he was sanding and said, "Only if you promise not to repeat last month's jam catastrophe."

Arya crossed her arms, mock-affronted. "It was abstract baking. You said it was edible!"

"I said I didn't die from it," he smirked.

She threw a kitchen towel at him, laughing. That was Arya—brilliant, unpredictable, always a little messy, and entirely magnetic.

In contrast, Arjun was an ordered personified. Archery was not a hobby; it was a ritual. Discipline, repetition, perfection—he lived and breathed it. Arya danced through life with curiosity, while he moved with focus.

And yet, nine months ago, their worlds had collided at the Focus Archery Club. Arya had joined impulsively after watching *Brave,* stayed long enough to shoot one accurate arrow, and left behind a memory—her laugh, wild and forgiving even when she missed.

Their first conversation had unfolded over a snapped bowstring and a mango popsicle. As he repaired her bow in silence, she casually recited a poem she had written the night before—about mangoes, heartbreak, and lunar eclipses. He did not say much, but her words stayed lodged in his mind.

From there, something bloomed—unexpected and unhurried.

Nine months later, Arjun was preparing for the Asian Games. Arya remained a hurricane of creativity, starting her own podcast, painting half a sunflower mural, and attempting to train a parrot to say, "Arya's awesome." The parrot instead screamed "Aarya sossum!" at odd hours.

But things had started to shift. Arjun had become more withdrawn. His phone stayed silent longer, and his replies were clipped. Arya tried not to mind—until that Friday evening.

She had spent the whole day embroidering a good-luck patch: a sunflower in the curve of a bow. She showed up at his archery range, smiling.

He did not look up from his practice.

"You're here," he said flatly.

She held up the patch. "A lucky charm. Handmade."

He glanced at it, then back at his arrows. "That's sweet. But I'm in the middle of something. Trials are soon."

She blinked. "That's all you're going to say?"

He sighed. "Arya, I can't afford distractions right now."

Her heart dropped. "That's what I am? A distraction?"

"You're not. But this—us—it's unpredictable. I need structure right now."

"You think love comes with a schedule?" she snapped.

"I think focus matters. I'm chasing something real."

She stepped back, stunned. "And I'm not real enough?"

"Arya, please don't twist this—"

"No. I get it. You don't have room for someone like me in your perfect, linear world. Maybe you never did."

She turned to leave.

"Arya, please don't do this."

She paused at the door, her voice breaking. "I already did."

The days that followed were hollow.

Arya stopped listening to her chaotic playlists. The pie idea was abandoned. Her parrot fell eerily silent, as though mourning with her. She deleted her podcast files and tore down her sunflower mural halfway through painting the second bloom.

Arjun, meanwhile, trained with mechanical precision. But something felt off. His grip wasn't steady. His arrows veered left. His trainer noticed.

"You're thinking too much," he said. "What changed?"

Arjun did not answer—but he knew.

Arya's absence was not just noticeable; it was deafening. No impulsive visits, no voice notes, no chaos at the edges of his silence.

He began checking his phone at night—wondering, waiting.

Two weeks later, a delivery arrived at Arjun's door.

Inside was a basket—the same one Arya had woven the previous winter. Inside it lay a perfectly ripe apple, a melted vanilla-scented candle, a napkin embroidered with a sunflower, and a folded letter.

"You were my calm, Arjun. But I see now that I was only noise to you. Maybe that's why you snapped.

But still, when I see apples, I think of you.

When I miss you, I bake.

I miss you every day.—A"

Arjun held the napkin for a long time before standing—quietly, resolutely.

It was a grey Sunday when Arya returned to the orchard—not to pick apples, just to walk. She missed the crisp scent of the leaves, the echo of shared laughter among the trees.

She did not expect to see him there.

But there he was—Arjun, bow slung over his back, holding the embroidered napkin in his hand.

"I read your letter," he said.

Arya swallowed. "You shouldn't have come. You have training."

"I have clarity."

She looked away. "So what now?"

He stepped closer. "I'm not good with mess. I thrive on routine. But you're the one beautiful mess I want in every part of my life."

Her lips trembled. "Even if I don't always stay in one lane?"

"You don't stay. You light up every lane you pass through. And I realised I would rather lose my balance with you than stay grounded without you."

She blinked, tears gathering. "Say that again."

He stepped forward and held her hand. "I miss you—every minute. I love your chaos. And I love you."

Arya exhaled, her breath shaky but relieved. "I burned the pie, by the way."

He smiled. "Then let's burn one together. For real this time."

That evening, the house once again smelled of cinnamon and second chances. Arya, back in her apple-print apron, hummed along to her chaotic playlist. Arjun helped peel apples—clumsily, but sincerely.

At dinner, the pie was imperfect. The crust was slightly too crisp, the vanilla ice cream too soft. But they ate it laughing.

Arjun handed her a box. Inside was a silver bracelet shaped like a bow, with a sunflower charm nestled in its curve.

"For the girl who doesn't stay still," he said.

She kissed his cheek. "From the boy who finally let go."

They lay on the rooftop again, hands entwined.

"You see constellations," she said.

"You see stories," he replied.

"We're not opposites."

"We're the bow and the breath," he whispered. "The stretch and the release."

She smiled, her head resting on his shoulder.

They were not perfect.

But they had found their own rhythm— sweet, messy, unforgettable.

Just like apple pie.

9

The Book- A Love Story

"Love often begins in a fleeting moment, yet its echo lingers, etched into the soul as a lifelong longing."

The college orientation hall buzzed with chatter and laughter—a mosaic of excitement and nervous anticipation. Tia scanned the room, gripping the strap of her bag, when her eyes met his. It was a glance that lasted a heartbeat too long, yet felt infinite. Viren's eyes, dark and alert, held hers. In that fleeting second, her pulse quickened, her breath caught, and her fingers tightened around her bag as though it were an anchor.

After the introductions, high tea was served in the courtyard, where sunlight shimmered on the fountain and danced along the fluttering sarees of the faculty. Viren approached her, a shy smile playing on his lips. "Hi, I'm Viren."

Tia extended her hand. Their handshake lingered longer than politeness required, silent words passing between them, their eyes expressing what their voices could not. The moment was broken when Ria, Tia's best friend, tugged at her sleeve. "We should head to the hostel, Tia," she insisted.

Viren began, "What's your name?" but his words were swallowed by the crowd as Ria pulled Tia away.

By the end of the first week, the seniors began their customary "welcome rituals." Tia and Viren, along with a few others, were made to stand in a line, answering rapid-fire questions, singing snippets of songs, and performing light-hearted dares. Fate, mischievous as ever, seemed determined to pair them together.

"Ah, you two—Mr Physics and Ms Literature. Partners for the fresher's party skit," a senior declared with mock gravity. "From now on, wherever one goes, the other follows."

Tia rolled her eyes, but when she glanced at Viren, he grinned as though destiny itself had spoken.

During the icebreaker sessions, they were asked absurd questions.

"What's your favourite colour?" a senior asked.

"Blue," Viren replied.

"Blue," Tia echoed, surprised. Their eyes met, amused by the coincidence.

"What's your dream vacation spot?"

"Greece," Tia said.

"Greece," Viren repeated at the same moment, startling himself.

The seniors laughed at their synchrony, teasing, "Twin flames!" But the laughter faded into the background for Tia and Viren. Each answer revealed another shared layer—tastes, quirks, even a favourite poet. It was more than similarity; it felt like recognition, as though they had known each other long before they met.

Even when they were made to dance awkwardly or perform ridiculous dialogues, they slipped into an easy rhythm. Between tasks, their conversations deepened—books, films, fears, ambitions—each word drawing them closer.

By the time fresher's party rehearsals began, they were no longer strangers. They had become co-conspirators in laughter, confidants of whispered secrets, and, in some inexplicable way, reflections of each other—two souls quietly finding their mirror.

The evening before the event, rehearsals ran late. Most had already left, but Tia and Viren lingered in the empty auditorium, refining their lines and laughing at their mistakes.

As the lights dimmed to a soft amber glow, silence settled around them. Tia sat cross-legged on the stage, flipping through her script, while Viren lay beside her, staring at the ceiling as though searching for unspoken answers.

"Tia," he said softly, uncertainty in his voice.

"Yes?" she replied, brushing a strand of hair from her face.

"Do you ever feel like you've known someone forever, even if it's only been a few days?"

Her heart skipped. She wanted to dismiss it lightly, but his gaze held hers with quiet sincerity. "Yes," she whispered. "With you, it feels that way."

For a moment, silence hung heavy, filled with words unsaid. Viren's fingers brushed against hers—tentative, yet deliberate. She did not pull away. Their eyes met, holding the weight of everything unspoken.

Tia parted her lips, courage rising—but just then, the auditorium doors burst open. Ria's voice rang out, "There you are! Still here? Come on, the hostel warden will lock the gate soon!"

The moment shattered—fragile, unfinished. They stood quickly, their hands slipping apart. Yet as they walked out beneath the twilight sky, both carried the same quiet certainty: something had begun.

The next morning, Tia wandered into the campus bookstore with Ria. The scent of fresh pages wrapped around her as her fingers drifted across the shelves. Then she found it—*The God of Small Things*, a first edition, the author's signature gleaming faintly on the page. Her heart raced. She clutched it, only to be told that the last copy had just been sold.

Disappointed, she traced the cover one last time before leaving, unaware that its new owner was already entwined with her life.

That evening, the fresher's party transformed the hall into a whirl of lights, music, and laughter. Tia searched the crowd until she found Viren. He wasn't in formal attire, but he held a book in his hand. Her breath caught.

He walked up to her, his eyes warm yet tinged with something deeper.

"I want you to have this," he said softly. "It's yours. Don't forget to read the last page—I've written something for you."

He handed her the book—the same one she had seen that morning—*The God of Small Things*.

Before she could respond, Ria swept her onto the dance floor. The music surged, lights blurred, and in the chaos, Tia searched for him—but he was gone.

The next morning, she learned that Viren had left for the National Defence Academy. His acceptance letter had arrived late. The news struck her like a sudden chill. There had been no goodbye—no chance to say what lingered in her heart.

Then she remembered the book.

But it was gone—lost in the noise and confusion of the previous night, swallowed by celebration.

Years passed. Tia travelled the world, wrote stories, and earned recognition, yet a quiet ache remained. Every copy of *The God of Small Things* she collected—seven in total—reminded her of the one she had lost. Still, she searched: in old bookshops, thrift stores, and forgotten shelves.

Then one ordinary afternoon, a message from Ria changed everything:

"You won't believe what I found in Mom's old bookshelf. Call me!"

Tia's pulse quickened as she dialled. Ria's voice overflowed with excitement. "Tia, it's your book. And there's something inside—a note."

Her breath caught.

Days later, the package arrived. The cover felt familiar in her hands, the faint scent of old pages stirring buried memories. She opened to the last page.

There it was—Viren's handwriting.

Tia,

If you're reading this, it means I couldn't say goodbye the way I wanted to. Tomorrow, I leave for the National Defence Academy, but I cannot go without telling you what has been in my heart.

From the very first day, something about you stayed with me, like a quiet melody I could never forget. Every moment we shared—every word, every silence—became more precious than I ever dared admit.

I don't know where life will take us, or if our paths will ever cross again. But what I feel for you will travel with me—in every march, every dawn, every star I look at in the night sky.

Yours,

Viren

Tears blurred her vision. Beneath his signature, she noticed something more—a phone number, faintly scribbled, followed by a single line: *Call me if you feel the same.*

Though decades had passed, something within her compelled her to dial.

The phone rang.

A gentle voice answered. "Hello?"

"I—I'm sorry… is this Viren's number?" she asked, her voice trembling.

"Yes, this was my son's home number," the voice replied. "Who is this?"

"My name is Tia. I… I knew Viren in college. He gave me a book. I only just found it."

A long silence followed.

Then the voice softened. "Tia… he used to speak about you. When he returned from the academy, he asked if you had called. He kept waiting… every time."

Tears streamed down her face. "I didn't know… I've been searching for him—for this book. I'm so sorry."

"He loved you," the woman continued gently. "Even when he went to serve, he carried you in his heart. Before leaving for the front lines during the Kargil War, he told me, 'If anything happens, tell Tia I loved her. Tell her I was always waiting.'"

Tia's breath faltered. "He… he died?"

"Yes," she replied softly. "He was martyred during the Kargil War. The nation honoured him, but to me, he was my son—a boy in love, waiting for a call that never came."

Tia clutched the book to her chest, overwhelmed by a love that had endured time, distance, and even death.

That night, she wrote with a fervour she had never known, pouring her heart into a story that had always been hers. She titled it *Whispers of Unspoken Love*—a tribute to Viren, who had loved her quietly and faithfully across time.

Months later, at the book launch, she shared their story with an audience moved by its depth and sorrow. Holding the book close, she whispered, "Viren, I'm sorry it took so long. But I hear you now."

And in the stillness of the empty hall, she felt his presence—enduring, eternal.

The book rested in her hands, a testament to a love that neither time nor fate could erase.

10

The Missed Call

Rashmi clutched the leather-bound journal as the taxi slowed before a moss-covered gate. Rain traced silver lines across the windshield, blurring the outline of a place that had once meant everything—or something she still could not name.

Visibility was poor. One headlight had failed, and on the slick road ahead, a truck lost control. Fate, it seemed, had already written its verdict in bold.

She did not notice the storm outside; her own was louder. This was not a birthday whim or a casual detour. It felt like an ending—or perhaps the beginning of chaos.

She had told Rishab, her husband, that she was attending a school workshop in Mumbai. It was a lie she had rehearsed well. In truth, she was in Bangalore, on her way to meet the man who had once made her feel seen. She had often wondered: was that love, or simply the relief of no longer feeling invisible?

Months had passed since Satish last replied to her messages. His silence had become familiar, almost like a second skin. Still, she called him—once, then again.

No answer.

Satish watched her name flash on his phone like an unfinished sentence. He sighed and turned it face down. "I'll call later," he murmured. But he never did.

The rain thickened, as if the sky itself was trying to warn her.

The crash came in an instant. Metal collided, glass shattered, and the taxi crumpled beneath the truck's weight. When everything stilled, the driver was already gone.

Rashmi survived—barely. Unconscious, bruised, and bleeding, she was pulled out through the broken window by strangers. In her hands, she still clutched the soaked journal.

Her bag and wallet were lost in the wreckage. Her phone lay crushed on the road, its screen dark and lifeless.

It had all begun years ago in Chennai, without intention or permission. Rashmi's son, Rahul, was six then—the centre of her world. But Rishab had reduced love to duty: to provide, to protect, to endure—the slow, quiet decay of a marriage.

She met Satish on a monsoon afternoon at a literature festival. She was the keynote speaker; he, a brooding journalist with eyes that seemed to hold unfinished poems. An interview became a conversation, and a conversation deepened into something neither had planned.

Poetry became their language. Their disagreements—over politics, music, even faith—turned into something charged and intimate.

With him, Rashmi shed her roles. She was no longer just a wife, a mother, a teacher. She was a woman rediscovering herself.

He once read her poem, *The Pause Between Us,* and faltered. That pause became their world.

They met in bookstores, lingered in the shelter of rain, exchanged books marked with hidden meanings. Yet Satish always kept a boundary—close enough to ignite, distant enough to deny, until distance was no longer enough.

The accident rewrote everything.

Rashmi awoke in a sterile hospital room with no memory of who she was. No name, no past—only a journal filled with blurred ink and fragments she could not understand.

At Bangalore General Hospital, she was recorded as "Unknown Female, Mid-30s." No phone, no identification, no one to claim her.

Satish assumed she had moved on. Rishab believed she was still in Mumbai.

A week later, her fingerprints matched her Aadhaar records. Her name was restored—but not her memories.

Rishab flew to Bangalore, carrying a storm within him. She was alive—injured, disoriented, but alive. He brought her home without question. Their son, Rahul, stood at the staircase, a toy airplane trembling in his hand.

"Mama?" he whispered.

Rashmi blinked. She recognised the warmth of the embrace, but not the meaning behind it. The house felt familiar, yet empty of memory. The bed, the life, even the man beside her—all felt distant.

Satish was nothing to her.

Perhaps forgetting is sometimes a form of mercy.

Rishab did not ask questions. Perhaps he already knew. Perhaps he welcomed the chance to begin again. He softened; she tried to become the person she was expected to be.

In another life, they might have been happy.

Satish, too, moved on. He married Gauri, a woman of quiet grace and sharp understanding. They had a daughter, Mahi. Yet even the most rooted lives carry shadows.

One evening, Gauri found an old photograph of Rashmi tucked away in a drawer. In the photograph, Rashmi was laughing in a café, unaware of the storms her smile had stirred. Gauri did not react with anger. She simply understood.

Some absences speak louder than presence.

The trip to Goa was Rishab's idea—a fresh start. Whether by chance or design, Satish and his family were there that same weekend in the same resort.

One morning, walking barefoot along the beach, Rashmi noticed a man watching her.

"Do I know you?" she asked.

He nodded slowly. "Chennai. Years ago."

She smiled, polite but distant. "I don't remember much from then. Not after the accident." And she walked away.

Satish remained where he was, suspended like a comma waiting for a sentence that would never follow.

That night, the ocean roared. He walked along the shore alone, phone in hand, whispering her name as though the tide might carry it back to her.

Upstairs, Rashmi sat beside her sleeping son, flipping through her journal. A pressed bougainvillaea petal slipped from between the pages. She smiled, though she did not know why.

Perhaps some loves are meant to exist only as absence—not in presence, but in the quiet ache of what could have been.

In a drawer back home, Satish kept a ring—bought in a moment of impulse, meant for a woman who existed only in fragments and metaphors.

He never gave it.

Some missed calls are not accidents; they are moments when fate hesitates—when doors almost open, but never do.

Rashmi never remembered.

Satish never forgot.

And life, as it always does, moved on—under separate skies, with hearts that once touched.

Almost.

11

Ghost Traces of Love

The rain tapped softly against the glass, like a persistent memory that refused to fade. Ananya barely noticed. She was absorbed in the glow of her phone, scrolling through reels that felt like fragments of other people's perfect lives—bridal showers adorned with pastel balloons, laughter captured in flawless frames, toddlers tumbling into arms that were not hers. Each clip pressed against her like a bruise, deepening her loneliness.

Then—ping.

Karan Arora has sent you a friend request.

Her breath caught.

Karan—the boy from high school she had loved in secret, whose name she had doodled in the margins of her notebooks, whose absence had stretched into years of silence.

Her finger trembled before she tapped accept.

Almost instantly, a message appeared.

Karan: Hey, stranger. Guess who's back?

Ananya: The prodigal son returns?

Karan: Took me a while to find you. You don't make it easy.

Ananya: Or maybe you didn't look hard enough.

Karan: Touché.

She laughed, surprised at herself. It felt like sunlight entering a house that had been shut for too long.

And just like that, they were back.

In the first few weeks, Karan was everywhere. Her phone lit up before dawn with Good morning, Anu. At night, he sent long voice notes—his voice low and warm, weaving into her half-sleep. He brought back memories she thought had long faded, as if he had been waiting just outside her life all these years.

He remembered things she had forgotten: how she won a poetry contest in Class IX with a poem about rain, how she dipped fries into strawberry milkshakes at the café near school, how she once said she wanted to write a book that "felt like holding someone's hand in the dark."

He teased her gently, called her Anu in a way no one else did, and sent her songs with captions like, *This reminded me of you.* Sometimes he asked about her pain, but never pressed. He simply listened, murmuring, "I wish I had been there."

The intimacy grew quickly—dangerously. He texted between meetings, during flights, even from noisy bars: Can't believe I finally have you back in my life.

For Ananya, who had always felt slightly invisible, the attention was intoxicating. Her fingers trembled when his name appeared on her screen. Her nights felt incomplete without his goodnight. She began writing again, scribbling poems on the backs of grocery bills, her words alive with new fire.

She felt seen, chosen, special.

She was falling.

But the cracks appeared quietly.

One night, he promised, I'll call you at ten, I swear. She brewed coffee and waited. Ten passed. Midnight slipped into two a.m. The phone remained silent. She lay awake, anxious and restless.

At dawn, she saw his story—neon lights, a bar, his arm slung around laughing friends. Crazy night!

When she confronted him, he replied, "Sorry, Anu! Lost track of time. I'll make it up to you."

And at first, he did—apologies, affection, attention. She forgave him.

But the pattern continued. Plans were made, and then broken. She was promised to be called, and then forgotten. He would disappear for days, only to return as though nothing had changed.

Karan: You know how work is.

Ananya: You had time to post from Bali.

Karan: Come on. That was work—with a little fun. Don't overthink.

Every concern of hers was dismissed with a laugh, a soft you're too sensitive, and a distant pat on the head.

He was everywhere—on beaches, at rooftop parties, at family gatherings, sipping wine in Spain, hiking in Patagonia. Everywhere except with her.

Nights turned into rituals of quiet hurt. She would sit at her desk, staring at an unfinished page, while the green dot beside his name glowed online. He was active—just not with her. Her fingers hovered over the keyboard, tempted to type hi, then withdrew, ashamed of needing so little.

Her book release came and went. What she had imagined as a moment of joy felt hollow. She had pictured his message, his call, his pride. Instead, there was silence.

Her phone buzzed repeatedly—colleagues, distant relatives, polite readers. Each time, hope flared, only to fade. She refreshed her notifications again and again.

His name never appeared.

She smiled it off in public, but alone, the absence pressed heavily on her. The book lay on her desk, its cover glowing under soft light—her achievement, her offering. Yet the one person she wanted to notice had vanished.

The next day, she saw his post online: Loved this piece by @randomwriter. Brilliant stuff.

Her chest tightened.

He had time for strangers, but not for her.

Ananya: You didn't even notice my book launch.

Karan: Oh shit, Anu! I saw it—just got caught up. Congrats! Super proud.

Ananya: You always see too late.

Karan: You're overthinking again.

But if work consumed him so completely, how did he find time for Europe, for parties, for endless celebrations?

Her grief was quiet. It seeped into her poems, into the silence of her room, into the untouched cups beside her bed.

The cycle repeated—intensity followed by absence, promises followed by silence. He would vanish for weeks, and then return casually: Miss me?

Ananya: Not really.

Karan: Ouch. That was cold.

Ananya: Not cold. Honest.

Karan: You know you mean a lot to me.

Ananya: If I did, I wouldn't have to remind you I exist.

Three dots appeared, and then vanished.

Karan: You don't know the full story.

Ananya: Then tell me.

Karan: I can't. Not now.

Ananya: Not now, or not ever?

Karan: Some ghosts shouldn't be touched.

And just like that—silence.

He was online. Posting. Living. Everywhere except with her.

She told herself not to care. But her body remembered. Her hands still reached for her phone. Her heart still reacted to his name. Her poems still carried him.

Then she saw it clearly—the early intensity, the attention, the memories. It had all been a hook. He had drawn her in, and then grown careless, certain she would stay.

The pain was sharp, but beneath it lay something deeper—humiliation.

He had taught her to crave him, and then dismissed her for needing him. He called her sensitive for noticing what he withheld. He made her feel like her love was excessive, while his neglect was normal.

It was heartbreak of the modern kind—intimacy built through screens, promises dissolved into silence, love measured in read receipts.

A year passed.

One night, as rain streaked her window, his message appeared again: Hey, stranger. Miss me?

Her fingers hovered. But something within her had changed.

Ananya: Not really.

She blocked him—not in anger, but in self-preservation.

The silence that followed was not empty. It was expansive, like a room finally filled with fresh air after years of suffocation.

For the first time in months, she turned to her desk. Her manuscript waited. She picked up her pen, her breath steady, her hand sure.

When her voice returned, it was quiet but resolute: I am not too much. I was never not enough. I was simply waiting for someone who was never coming.

The ink flowed, carrying the ache with it.

Karan's words lingered—Some ghosts shouldn't be touched.

Perhaps he was right. He had been a ghost all along—a presence that flickered but never truly existed beside her.

But she no longer needed to reach for that ghost.

She had her own story to write.

And in choosing herself, she found something steadier than attention, stronger than longing.

She found freedom.

The rain tapped gently on the glass again, but this time, she noticed.

For months, she had mistaken echoes for love, shadows for warmth. Now she understood.

A ghost may haunt—but it cannot hold.

And the rain no longer sounded like grief.

It sounded like a release.

12

The Roman Holiday

Lakshmi Aiyar's favourite film was *Roman Holiday*—not because she had a crush on Gregory Peck, but because it was the first movie she watched on a date with her newlywed husband, Dr Kartik Iyer. It was also her first English film.

Raised in the small, conservative town of Kalpathi in Palakkad, Lakshmi was the only girl from her *agraharam* (a traditional Tamil Brahmin settlement) to attend the Indian Institute of Science in Bangalore. Although her education in Biology brought her recognition, it did little to change her. Her values remained firm, her orthodox views unchallenged, and her quiet naivety intact. She accepted an arranged marriage soon after completing her studies, following a proposal from Kartik's parents.

Dr Kartik Iyer—"the Aiyer with an I," as Lakshmi teasingly called him—had been smitten with her ever since he first saw her on the IISc campus. While working toward his PhD in Physics, he often found excuses to pass by the Biology department just to catch a glimpse of her. He was fascinated by the intensity with which she immersed herself in her research on molluscs. Even though the queen conch on her table was merely a specimen, Kartik understood its cultural significance to a devout 'Tam-Bram' (a common nickname for Tamil Brahmins in Bangalore).

Their paths crossed often—at the canteen, along campus walkways, and during seminars—but Lakshmi never once noticed him. She remained entirely unaware of his existence.

At an international conference on campus, Lakshmi presented a paper on hermit crabs. Kartik, despite having no real interest in the subject, attended the conference simply to watch her. So deep was his admiration that, without ever speaking to her, he decided she was the woman he would marry—no matter how hard her shell was to crack.

Kartik was Lakshmi's complete opposite—adaptable, adventurous, and full of life. Soon after their marriage, he secured a postdoctoral position at the University of Trieste in Italy. For Lakshmi, moving abroad felt like stepping into an entirely different world. She clung to her Indian identity, refusing to change her attire or habits. Kartik watched with quiet amusement as she stubbornly held on to her customs. She avoided Italian food, dismissing it as bland, and steered clear of local wines and cheeses. Instead, she walked through cobbled streets in search of Indian stores to buy her beloved spices. Kartik eventually stopped suggesting culinary adventures.

One day, Lakshmi visited a beach in Trieste, her Kanjeevaram saree flowing in the breeze, paired with Kolhapuri sandals. When she saw women lounging in bikinis, she gasped and nearly fainted. Kartik, ever patient, explained that such sights were normal in Italy—and even in parts of India like Goa.

"Come out of your shell, my hermit crab," he teased. "See the world. Move with it. Enjoy it. When in Rome, do as the Romans do."

Flushed with embarrassment and irritation, Lakshmi stormed toward the waves, only to be drenched by a sudden surge of water. Humiliated, she hurried away—until she stepped on something beneath her sandal. Curious, she bent down and saw a crab emerging from its old exoskeleton.

She stood still, captivated, witnessing this rare process—moulting—felt almost surreal. It reminded her of her own research, where she had studied how crabs shed their shells not only because they outgrow them, but also to regenerate lost limbs. Watching the fragile creature struggle free, she found herself reflecting: change can be painful, but it can also lead to growth and renewal.

That Christmas, hoping to lift her spirits, Kartik planned a trip to Rome. Lakshmi had been homesick, and he had been busy with work. They were invited to a Christmas party at a colleague's home, and Kartik was scheduled to deliver a speech at a conference the following morning. Wanting to surprise her, he bought her a white fur coat and stylish boots for the chilly weather.

But when it came time to pack, Lakshmi remained as resolute as ever. She chose a vibrant Kanjeevaram saree, adding only a shawl for warmth. When she emerged from the bathroom, her long hair cascading down her back, she looked radiant—almost divine. Kartik, however, sighed at her stubbornness, glancing at the untouched coat and boots.

"You do know there's a ballroom dance tonight, right?" he said lightly. "Every couple is expected to join. But if you're not up for it, my colleague Reshma can take your place."

Lakshmi raised an eyebrow. "Reshma? You never mentioned her."

"She joined last week," he replied casually. "She dances well—and she'd certainly appreciate the coat and boots. It will be such a waste otherwise. You loved Audrey Hepburn's outfit in *Roman Holiday*, remember? I bought these for you. But if you don't want them, I'll send them to her."

Without waiting for a response, he handed the package to the butler, instructing him to deliver it to Miss Reshma, who was staying nearby. Lakshmi said nothing.

That evening, Kartik arrived early at the party. The mansion was beautifully decorated, and the air was filled with the aroma of Italian cuisine. As he stood enjoying a slice of pizza, his attention was drawn to a striking woman entering the room. She wore a sleek black dress, paired with the very coat and boots he had bought.

Kartik stared in disbelief. It was Lakshmi.

"My God… I can't believe it's you!" he exclaimed.

Lakshmi smiled, a hint of mischief in her eyes, as she picked up a glass of wine from a passing waiter. "Well," she said, twirling slightly so the coat flared around her, "when in Rome, do as the Romans do."

"I've been asked to dance by your colleague, Alessandro Bianchi," she added playfully. "He reminds me a bit of Gregory Peck. So I thought—why not be Audrey Hepburn for a night? The coat and boots weren't wasted after all."

Kartik stood speechless as she raised her glass in a teasing toast. "Enjoy your time with Miss Reshma. I'll see you later."

With that, she glided across the ballroom, confident and graceful, to join Alessandro on the dance floor.

"Reshma? Who…?" Kartik muttered under his breath.

Watching her, he couldn't help but smile. His "hermit crab" had finally stepped out of her shell—and revealed a world of surprises he had never imagined.

13

My Frozen Beauty

I kicked off my boots, my wet socks clinging to my frozen feet, each step sending a sharp sting through my numbed toes. The wind howled outside, rattling the windows as if nature itself mourned with me. The fireplace loomed in the corner, its hearth dark, the once comforting scent of burning wood now a distant memory.

Frantically, I fumbled through the drawer of the old oak table, pulling out empty matchbooks, their promise of warmth long gone. With each failed attempt, a wave of helplessness settled over me. Shivering, I paced the room, avoiding the centre where something far colder than the air seemed to linger—the transport coffin.

Inside was my beloved Mukta lay frozen. Her body was sealed within the sterile casing meant for her final journey home. Her face, once a canvas of subtle expressions I struggled to interpret, was now still and lifeless, her skin as pale as the snow into which she had disappeared. Even in life, her emotions had been a mystery to me. I could never decipher the quiet moments when her lips trembled or the fleeting shadow of sorrow behind her eyes. I often felt like an outsider to her inner world, left guessing at her thoughts, even as she shed silent tears I failed to understand.

Yet my love for her was boundless. Perhaps I had failed to express it in a way she could grasp, lost in my own inability to articulate the depth of my feelings. We had always circled our fears and desires, both too guarded to truly share them. Still, I loved her with a fierce devotion. I longed to protect her from the very world she sought to conquer. Mukta was born to soar, her spirit too wild for the mundane. Every new adventure, every challenge, was her way of reaching for something greater than herself. She was always chasing the next horizon, the next feeling, while I remained earthbound, watching from a distance.

At times, she would scream—not out of anger, but from something deeper, something I never fully understood. Her voice would echo through the empty halls of our house, her anguish filling the spaces between us. The absence of children, the unfulfilled longing to create life, haunted her. She tried to fill that void with the world's wonders, immersing herself in strange pursuits, sometimes crossing unspoken boundaries. I was aware of some of her transgressions, yet I forgave her—every single time—because I knew her heart was searching for peace, for purpose.

Her final dream—the one that consumed her—was the Alps. She spent countless nights speaking of their beauty, their raw power, their promise of redemption. I knew she was not prepared. Her body was not strong enough, and she lacked the training. But when Mukta set her mind to something, there was no stopping her. I could not leave her side, even if it meant walking into her madness.

That morning, as I sat in the small hotel room, the firewood stacked neatly in the corner, a sense of unease settled within me. A report came in about a rare avalanche sweeping through the Alps. My stomach dropped. Mukta had left for her hike at dawn, her smile full of promise, her eyes lit with determination. Deep down, I knew—I had to find her.

I knew nothing about trekking or surviving in such harsh conditions, but it did not matter. She was out there, and I could not bear the thought of her calling for me while I sat idly by. The locals warned me, told me it was impossible to find anyone. Fifteen others had gone missing. None of it mattered. My heart led me; my love drove me forward. The snow swallowed me whole, my ill-suited boots sinking deep with each step. The thin air burned my lungs, yet I pressed on, my mind flickering in and out of clarity.

Then I saw her through the haze. She stood before me, her face radiant, glowing with warmth I had rarely seen. She was no longer the distant, unreadable woman I had known. She was alive, vibrant, calling to me. Her hand beckoned, and without hesitation, I followed. She led me to her resting place beneath the snow. My trembling hands worked feverishly, pushing aside the frozen layers until at last, I uncovered her.

Her face was blue, her body stiff. And yet, I felt it—she had waited for me. In those final moments, as the cold claimed her, she had held on, waiting for my arrival. She had known I would come.

Now, as she lay in the coffin, still and silent, she seemed almost at peace, as though the weight of the world had finally lifted from her shoulders. She had conquered the Alps. She had reached the summit, if only for a fleeting moment.

The room remained bitterly cold, my hands shaking from more than grief. Then I noticed a faint glint beneath the coffin—a lighter, half-buried under discarded blankets. My hands trembled as I lit the fire. Flames burst to life, crackling and hissing, their warmth spreading slowly through the room.

A soft golden glow fell across Mukta's face. She looked ethereal, like a queen in her icy repose.

For the first time, I found the words that had long remained unspoken.

"You are breathtakingly beautiful, my love."

And in that moment, with the firelight dancing around us, I felt her presence—not the distant, unknowable Mukta I had known, but the woman she had always been, waiting for me to truly see her.

14

In between the Seconds- A Delhi Layover

Aadi Ghosh did not walk. He whirred. Always a blur in motion, he lived out of Samsonite suitcases and Google Calendar pop-ups. A senior partner at a consulting firm that valued PowerPoint transitions over human emotions, Aadi treated layovers like coffee breaks and relationships like time zone incompatibilities.

At 38, he had more loyalty points than friends. His dating life was a montage of clinking glasses, half-hearted smiles, and ghosted follow-ups. He was not lonely, per se, just permanently in transit.

Meanwhile, across Delhi, Ranjini Mohan was not just in place; she was rooted. A freelance editor by paycheck and an unapologetic dreamer by destiny, she lived in a modest apartment filled with more characters than people. Her walls were plastered with scribbled quotes, her mugs mismatched, and her cat, Kafka, was convinced she was an existentialist.

She once went on a date and compared the man to Dostoevsky's duller cousin. He did not get the reference. They never met again.

Sometimes, on sleepless nights, she would flip through travel blogs and dream about Lisbon—its tiled alleyways, and bookstores older than empires. A city, she often thought, where stories might wait at café tables for those patient enough to listen.

Gate 27A, Indira Gandhi International Airport – Where Fates Misbehave

The announcement was cruel: "Flight to Istanbul delayed by 24 hours."

Aadi exhaled the kind of sigh that suggested capitalism had just personally betrayed him. His inbox was overflowing, three phones were buzzing, and his calendar was rearranging itself like an impatient Rubik's cube.

"Aw, poor boardroom gladiator," came a voice to his left, doused in dry wit and chamomile empathy.

He turned.

She was in a crumpled cotton kurta the colour of misplaced poetry, thermos in hand, eyebrows arched like quotation marks.

"Excuse me?" he blinked, mid-email, thumb hovering above *send*.

"Sorry," she said, sipping, "you just looked like someone who was about to sue the weather."

Aadi's laugh came out sharp, unplanned, almost suspicious. "And you look like someone who knitted that thermos a sweater."

"I did. It's called commitment. You wouldn't understand."

"Touché."

The terminal buzzed with luggage wheels and announcements, but in that suspended moment, it felt oddly hushed.

They wandered to a nearby airport café. It had sterile lighting softened by the comfort of brewing coffee. Steam curled from cups, and the window overlooked the tarmac where aircraft wings gleamed like tired birds.

She opened her notebook, its cover crowded with doodles and coffee stains. "I was supposed to finish my novel's epilogue tonight," she said, twirling her pen.

"Deadline?" he asked, clicking open his laptop.

"Dreamline," she corrected, with a grin that disarmed him.

He smirked, pulling up his Google Calendar anyway, a neat grid of future cities. "Meetings, flights, workshops… rinse and repeat."

"You make life sound like a laundromat."

"Sometimes it feels like one," he admitted.

One coffee became two. Two became parathas by the Yamuna, the air tinged with monsoon dampness and roasted corn from roadside vendors. They sat on a stone ledge, watching the river move with the patience of centuries.

"Ever read *The Little Prince*?" she asked suddenly, pulling out a tattered copy.

"Is that the fox one?"

"It's the everything one."

Her fingers traced underlined passages as if they were braille meant only for her. He caught himself leaning closer, not to read, but to listen.

Later, at Daryaganj's Sunday book market, they wandered between towers of yellowed paperbacks and old Urdu poetry collections. She picked up a volume of the Brontës.

"Charlotte was dramatic," she declared.

"She had flair!" he countered.

"Anne was subtle."

"You mean invisible."

Their argument split into laughter, their voices echoing among piles of forgotten books, watched over by indifferent pigeons.

By dusk, she dragged him into a narrow shop with flickering neon lights: a tattoo parlour.

"Are you serious?" he asked, tugging at his cufflinks.

"Deadly. Some moments deserve ink."

His tattoo: *Wanderer.*

Hers: *Wonderer.*

"Do you plan these things?" he asked, half amused, half shaken by his own compliance.

"I write these things," she grinned, bandaging her arm.

They ended the night at a rooftop café strung with fairy lights. Delhi lay sprawled beneath them—honking, glowing, alive. She nursed her chai, and he his overpriced mint tea.

Aadi's blazer was crisp, his shoes polished, his watch limited edition. But his voice trembled when he finally spoke.

"I don't know if I'm happy," he confessed, staring at the swirling leaves in his tea. "I have everything, don't I? Corner office, platinum status, calendars booked for months. My passport has more stamps than my memory has moments. But when I go home, if I even call it that, it's just a furnished apartment and silence that doesn't even bother greeting me anymore."

He paused and then met her gaze. "Sometimes I wonder if I've outsourced my entire life. Delegated love, rescheduled joy, postponed meaning. I'm tired of running rooms. I just don't know how to sit still."

She did not rush to fill the silence. Only after a long moment did she murmur, "I spend my days writing about love, the grand kind, the aching kind, the kind that waits at train stations or sends letters from warzones. But me? I've never stayed long enough for breakfast. I always leave before the sun, and the silence asks too many questions."

Their honesty hovered like incense smoke. It was fragile, fragrant, impossible to ignore.

At dawn, they returned to Gate 27A, bags heavier, hearts lighter.

"Will I see you again?" he asked, voice low, almost unpractised in its sincerity.

She smiled, a curve of lips that held both ache and courage. "Maybe. If destiny misses its flight again."

She handed him a Polaroid: both of them laughing under Qutub Minar, sun in their eyes, silence in their future. On the back, she had written:

In another life, I'll write you a story where we have more time.

Then she was gone, vanishing into the security line like the final chapter of a book you never wanted to finish.

Aadi flew to Istanbul, 24 hours late for a board meeting that happened without him.

The world did not crumble. In fact, he was not even missed.

Something shifted.

He cancelled back-to-back trips, took walks without AirPods, bought a typewriter he did not know how to use and posted photos of empty park benches and foggy windows with no hashtags.

He started journaling. His assistant thought he had joined a mindfulness cult.

And once—just once—he caught himself missing a connecting flight on purpose.

Ranjini finally finished her novel. It was about a man who never stopped moving and a woman who never left. But both met when time sat down for tea.

She titled it: *In Between the Seconds.*

It was quietly published. No fanfare. No viral reels. But it reached quiet corners of hearts that knew exactly what it meant to love briefly but fully.

The last chapter ended not with a kiss, but with a question, a puzzle piece.

The clue was simple—a riddle hidden in plain sight:

If you're reading this in a city where books get second chances and baklava isn't just dessert,

Look under the fox in Chapter Seven.

I've left a key in the footnote.

Lisbon, Two Years Later

Aadi stood near a bookstore waiting for a client meeting at a neighbourhood café tucked in an alley that smelled of cinnamon and serendipity. The meeting got cancelled at the last minute.

He was not looking for the book. Not consciously.

The window display caught his eye—the unusual cover, the familiar name. The title stole his breath.

He turned the pages with trembling fingers, laughing at their inside jokes tucked in metaphors and chapter names.

And then he saw it—Chapter Seven – The fox.

The footnote read:

For the one who once wandered through my Tuesday—

I'll be at Café Alecrim, Rua das Flores, every June 10th.

Order the masala chai. I'll come find you.

He closed the book, pulse steadying into something dangerously like hope.

The barista looked up. "Would you like anything, sir?"

"Yes," Aadi smiled, placing the book down like a love letter that had finally found its address.

"Masala chai, please. Hot. With no delay."

The café was small, the kind where wooden chairs creaked with memory and walls held stories in chipped paint. Outside, Lisbon's Rua das Flores glowed in late-afternoon light—balconies spilling geraniums, Fado drifting from an unseen guitar. Inside, the air smelled of cinnamon and cardamom, as if time itself had steeped in the pot.

He sat by the window, palms resting against the warm porcelain of his chai, and waited. Minutes stretched like hesitant sentences. He traced circles on the table and tried not to look at the door whenever it opened.

A little boy ran in, clutching a balloon. A couple whispered over pastries. A tourist asked for directions. Each face was not hers, and yet his heart leapt anyway.

The chai cooled. His fingers drummed the rim of the cup. Aadi wondered, had he misread it? Was the riddle just a metaphor, not a map? Was this another layover in the story of someone who never stayed?

And then—

The door chimed softly.

She walked in wearing a linen dress the colour of quiet mornings, hair a little shorter, eyes exactly the same. A canvas tote hung from her shoulder, which had her own book cover printed in vibrant colours. It was stuffed with books and mismatched notebooks. And there it was, the same battered thermos, still dressed in its knitted sweater, dangling from the bag like an old joke that had never stopped being funny.

For a heartbeat, she did not see him. She was scanning the counter, murmuring something to the barista. But when she finally turned, their eyes caught. The café stilled, as if Lisbon itself had agreed to hold its breath.

Ranjini's lips curved into that bittersweet smile that had once dismantled him at Gate 27A, Indira Gandhi International Airport, New Delhi. "So," she said softly, approaching his table, "you ordered the right thing."

Aadi laughed, shaky and unguarded, every flight he had ever taken collapsing into this one arrival.

"I was afraid you'd be late," he managed.

She set her bag down, the thermos thudding gently against the chair. As she pushed her sleeve up, the tattoo peeked out—*Wonderer*—slightly faded but intact. Aadi's own wrist, almost reflexively, itched beneath his cuff where *Wanderer* lived. Two halves of the same impulsive night, reunited after years of silence.

"I told you once," she said, pulling out a notebook, "some moments deserve ink. This one deserved more."

He leaned forward, eyes searching hers. "Tell me… why June 10th? Why is that date in your book?"

Ranjini smirked, that half-playful, half-secretive curve of her lips. "Because it's my birthday. The day I celebrated with a stranger at an airport after missing a flight, just two years ago."

The words lingered between them, not heavy, but glowing. Like a candle finally lit after waiting too long.

Outside, Lisbon moved on. Trams rattling, vendors calling, music spilling into cobblestones. But for Aadi and Ranjini, time finally sat down for tea.

15

Coded in Love, Written in Longing

December in Chennai shimmered not with snow, but with fairy lights draped like whispers along palm trees and apartment balconies. There was a deceptive chill in the air, not enough for sweaters, but just enough to hint that the year was quietly winding down. Inside a towering glass-panelled office building in Tidal Park near Taramani, the air-conditioning hummed too loudly for a Friday evening.

Raagesh stared at the envelope on his desk.

It was thick, cream-coloured and embossed with the company logo.

It was a letter of promotion with an offer in Singapore. It was simply prestige in bold letters, a title strung with an extra syllable, fattened with borrowed importance, a salary padded with zeroes like confetti on a spreadsheet.

It was everything Raagesh had burnt his midnight oil for – Five relentless years of spreadsheets over sunsets, takeaways over tables, and power naps stolen between strategy calls. There were weeks he could not tell Thursday from Sunday. Even bio breaks had become a luxury.

And now, his reward lay inside a cream-coloured envelope, its corners slightly curled, as if even the paper knew it had arrived too late because something else had arrived before it, something softer, warmer.

Moumita was a writer from Kolkata. They had come across a late-night assignment. She was editing a heritage column; he was debugging a report. What began as a shared frustration over a clunky document soon became the slow unravelling of souls across screens.

Moumita was not just from Kolkata, she was Kolkata! A walking, breathing ode to yellow taxis, Shyamalal tea stalls, old bookstores on College Street, and the way Howrah Bridge sighed under the weight of dusk.

Oxford had sent her an offer too, once—an internship in journalism and creative writing. But she had turned it down with a shrug and a line Raagesh would never forget.

"Too cold, too polished. I can't live in a place where fish means just fish and chips. And their smiles don't reach the eyes."

So she stayed in Kolkata, in his inbox, in his thoughts.

And just like that, the glossy skyline of Singapore lost its shine because something far rarer had happened.

He had fallen in love not just with a woman, but with a city he had never visited, through the metaphors she lived in.

"Congrats, man! Singapore, huh? You cracked it," a colleague grinned, clapping him on the shoulder.

He nodded vaguely, with a hollow smile.

The letter was kept back in the envelope. It looked like it had never been opened.

When the floor thinned out for the Christmas weekend, he stayed behind. The silence felt honest. He clicked open his internal dashboard and, with a few deliberate keystrokes, approved a transfer to his company's Kolkata branch.

No upward movement, no celebration, Just a lateral shift, geography over ambition.

He closed the laptop, took a deep breath, and looked out at the evening skyline.

"She'll be surprised," he whispered, almost unsure.

But what if she wasn't?

In Kolkata, the sky hung heavy with the smell of roasted peanuts, nostalgia, and a peculiar kind of stillness—the kind that arrives when change tiptoes in, disguised as dusk.

Moumita stood outside her favourite tea café in Gariahat, fingers curled around a kullad of slightly too cold Darjeeling tea. Normally, that earthy aroma calmed her. Today, it only reminded her that her hands were trembling.

Inside her tote bag, folded neatly between a Murakami paperback and a packet of elaichi, was a resignation letter with her ink still wet on it. She had stared at it for an hour before signing, as if her pen were a blade and she were slicing off a part of herself.

Tomorrow, she would board a flight to Chennai.

Not for a job.

Not for a promotion.

Not even for a new beginning, technically.

But for him.

The man who never once said *'come,'* but in every conversation made her feel she already belonged.

"You're really doing this?" Asha, her roommate of four years, asked, sitting on the bed, legs crossed, chewing on a pen cap, as Moumita zipped her suitcase slowly and deliberately.

"I've never been more unsure about anything," Moumita had grinned, "which is exactly why I know it's right."

The grin had cracked a little at the edges, but she did not let it fall.

She had not told Raagesh. Not directly.

She was never good with declarations.

She preferred metaphors, suggestion, the way Tagore would write about rain and mean longing.

So she had planned to give him a hint – A quiet signal. A little Moumita-style mayhem, as her college friends would call it.

In her bag were things absurd, poignant, and deeply, unmistakably hers:

A red-and-white stole, "for the Chennai winter," she had joked to herself, knowing well it would sit untouched; a box of sandesh her mother insisted on making, as if sweetness could seal decisions; a brass kuthu vilakku lamp she had bought after haggling like a banshee in Kalighat—"for spiritual aesthetic and Instagram," she told Asha.

A hand-lettered bookmark she had made late last night, shaking slightly as she inked the quote: *"Whatever you're looking for won't come in the form you expect." — Murakami.* She hoped he would find it tucked inside the book she once recommended. She hoped he would understand

Moumita had never chased career ladders. She chased meaning. She knew it made her look non-serious in a world obsessed with credentials, but she also knew Oxford would never understand the language of *adda* or the sacred joy of *jhalmuri* eaten during tram rides.

"You're giving up everything for a man?" Asha had asked again, concern laced in sarcasm.

"No," Moumita had replied quietly. "I'm choosing someone who feels like home. I just hope his home has room for me."

And now, as the streetlight flickered above her and the smell of someone roasting peanuts mixed with the warmth of old Hindi songs floated from a shop nearby, Moumita took a deep breath.

Every heartbeat thudded like a stubborn tabla rhythm: *What if he doesn't feel the same? What if I'm a paragraph in his life, and he's already on the next chapter? What if Chennai is too hot, too fast, too different?*

But another voice, deeper and far more unreasonable, whispered back: *What if he's standing there, confused but smiling, waiting—just as unsure, just as terrified?*

She smiled faintly, took one last sip from the kullad, and muttered, "Let the city take care of me till tonight."

Then she crushed the empty clay cup gently in her hands. The ritual now over, she walked into the evening, carrying Kolkata in her breath and a thousand unspoken hopes in her bag.

It all started with a tweet during the July monsoon.

@MouWrites: *"Love is a language even silence speaks."*

@RaageshRants: *"But silence doesn't return HTTP 200."*

She laughed aloud. Alone. Surprised by the burst of joy.

A minute later, her DMs blinked.

"Couldn't resist. Midnight debugging. Your tweet hit different."

"You're forgiven. It was a beautiful punchline."

And that was it.

Weeks passed in an addictive haze of late-night chats.

They argued about algorithms and alliteration. She taught him haiku; he explained recursion. She mailed him a used copy of *Gitanjali*. He sent her a Spotify playlist titled *"Songs for Syntax."*

On stormy nights, during a long power cut, she read to him, *The Grapes of Wrath,* slowly and deliberately.

She called him "Byte Boy." He called her "Bookmark."

No one used the word love.

But it slipped in anyway.

By mid-September, Raagesh's fridge looked like a language lab.

Sticky notes:

Jol – water

bhalo bashi – love

mach – fish

His Bengali neighbour caught him one night swearing over a smoking pan.

"You trying to burn Bengal?" she teased.

"I'm trying to cook *alu posto,*" he muttered.

She laughed so hard that she nearly dropped her groceries and then invited him over and showed him the art of *panch phoron*—the Bengali 5-spice tadka.

Meanwhile, Moumita watched Tamil YouTubers to mimic intonation. She read Perumal Murugan aloud to herself. She practised saying *"thanni venum"* with the right lilt.

She mapped every beach in Chennai on Google Maps and marked her favourite: *"Future walks with him."*

They were both trying to be fluent in each other, but said nothing about it.

Two weeks before Christmas, Moumita sent a message late at night:

"Hope you're not gone far when I get there."

It was her version of a hint. Her voice was behind the curtain.

Raagesh read it, smiled, and replied: *"Never too far."*

She interpreted it as an affirmation. He took it as a metaphor.

They were inches from the truth, yet on separate maps.

That weekend, their chats grew sparse. One missed call, one unsent meme, and excuses of being busy, yet their hearts thudded louder.

They both felt it – The edge of something beautiful or devastating. But neither asked, neither dared.

Raagesh landed in Kolkata on Christmas Eve.

The air smelled of roasted peanuts and winter fog, and every auto horn felt like it was announcing him to her.

He took the long way to Gariahat, just to pass the bookstore she had once sent him a photo of.

In his duffel were three things: A printed Tagore quote on thick handmade paper, a tiffin of *kosha mangsho* he had cooked, following the recipe of his neighbour, and a bottle of her favourite jasmine perfume.

The staircase to her flat groaned under his steps. He wiped his palms on his jeans before knocking.

The door opened to an old woman with clouded eyes.

"She left this morning," she said. "Got a job in Chennai. She was a very sweet girl, used to smile a lot."

For a second, the words made no sense. He stood there, the tiffin warm against his palm, as if it could keep him from going cold inside. The steam curled upward, disappearing into the December air. His throat clenched around all the words he had rehearsed.

Somewhere far across the country, Moumita stood outside a quiet Chennai apartment. Her red stole caught in the sea breeze.

She cradled a tin of sandesh like it might melt if she breathed too hard.

The watchman looked up, adjusting his shawl.

"Saar left today. He said something about Kolkata and was smiling like he'd just found gold."

Her fingers went slack. The tin hit the tiles with a dull thud. Sweetness scattered in soft, collapsing pieces. She stared at them, broken sugar mirroring the fracture in her chest. She did not bend to pick it up.

That night, his message came first.

Raagesh: *"Landed in Kolkata. Took the transfer for you. Surprise ruined. Merry Christmas, Mou."*

A pause, and then came her reply.

Moumita: *"I'm in Chennai. Quit my job. Took one here for you. The new office starts Monday."*

Another pause and then:

Moumita: *"We're idiots. Beautiful, reckless, well-intentioned idiots."*

Her phone rang. It was a video call from Raagesh.

She answered, and for a long moment, they just looked at each other through the grainy video feed.

He was sitting on her doorstep in Kolkata, a Tagore quote in his lap. She was leaning against his Chennai gate, the empty tin still beside her.

Moumita (softly): "You learned Bengali?"

Raagesh (half-smile): "Enough to order mishti doi… and ruin poetry."

Moumita: "You gave up Singapore?"

Raagesh: "You gave up Oxford once. I get it now."

Silence. Not heavy — just full.

Moumita: "What if we met somewhere with no history? No ghosts?"

Raagesh: "Neutral ground? Build our own?"

Moumita: "Hyderabad?"

He lifted the Tagore card to the camera. She held up the red stole.

Neither of them said yes. They did not need to.

They moved to Hyderabad after a few months of staying in alien cities, learning that absence leaves scars even in places filled with charm. Kolkata haunted Raagesh terribly with its soul, Moumita. Chennai was never the same for Moumita without Raagesh's laughter to soften its edges.

Hyderabad felt like home instantly. They lived in a flat with more windows than walls, letting in sunlight like forgiveness.

The first week was messy. Furniture deliveries were running late, one mattress was being shared on the floor, and arguments over curtains versus blinds were breaking out. They burnt their first attempt at biryani together, then laughed until tears fell, ordering *pani puri* from the street corner to fill their stomachs.

Raagesh took up tech freelancing.

Moumita launched her blog: *Letters Between Cities.*

Her debut book – *The Missed Call* – A story of two people, one mistake and the miracle of second chances.

They married on a December rooftop under a sky full of toy planes.

Every Christmas Eve, they hosted a gathering called *'The Almost Meeting'*.

They served *kosha mangsho* and *rasam,* read love letters and debug life, hung the red stole like a curtain by the balcony, and kept the unopened promotion envelope tucked in a drawer, not as regret, but as proof of choice.

Two tiny planes traced the maps of Kolkata and Chennai.

Two hearts that once flew in opposite directions.

And finally landed.

Together.

16

The Lost Word

Mussoorie was colder than Ayaan remembered.

The December wind slipped through his woollen coat and settled along his spine like an old, unresolved memory. The hills lay draped in layers of mist, as though time itself had been folded carefully and tucked into the valley. The scent of pine, dew, and distant bonfires drifted through the air—a familiar perfume that made the years he had carefully sealed away spill open again.

He felt the weight of twenty-five winters—some gentle, most harsh—pressing against his chest.

As he climbed the stone steps to the old library, he paused. This was where he and Maya had once hidden—from tedious lectures, from the world, from themselves. The brass plaque at the entrance had faded to a weary bronze, but Ayaan's heartbeat, traitor that it was, still stumbled like a young boy's.

The official reason for his return was the alumni reunion.

The truth was quieter.

He had come to find her - Maya, his almost-confession, his almost-home, his almost-forever.

She had always carried poetry in her pockets and sunlight in her eyes. She scribbled verses on receipts, newspaper scraps, even tissue paper, handing them to him like tiny detonations of feeling. He would pretend to critique them academically, but in truth, he memorised every curve of her handwriting.

Maya brought the world to life around her. She awakened something in him, too—"dream louder, write more, love deeper," she would say in her half-laughing voice. And he would stand there, wanting—aching—to tell her that she was the only sentence he never needed to rewrite.

But courage was a language he never learned.

Ayaan remembered everything:

The nervous swivel of her ankle,

The way she chewed pencil tips like secrets,

The tune of old Hindi songs she hummed unconsciously.

And one evening—oh, that evening—when her shoulder brushed his, and she lingered a heartbeat longer than necessary.

He should have spoken.

He did not.

He believed gestures could compensate for silence, that she would understand without him having to say the words aloud. But love, even when it burns brightly within, must be expressed to be known.

Life moved on with quiet efficiency. They graduated. They drifted apart. And silence, once a seed, grew into a forest.

Years later, he saw her in Delhi at a book launch. She wore an ivory saree—simple, elegant, devastating. Beside her stood a man whose eyes followed her the way unfinished poems follow their poet.

The wedding ring was small, but it struck him like an avalanche.

He left without speaking to her—again.

And for the next two decades, he lived with the ghost of everything he had never said.

So when the reunion invitation arrived, with *Mussoorie* written in elegant calligraphy, something within him whispered: *Go.*

Not to reclaim anything—only to lay to rest a chapter that had never truly begun.

He saw her standing by the old oak tree—the one where they had carved their initials, but only halfway, because neither had the courage to complete the heart around them.

Her hair now carried streaks of silver that glimmered in the mist. Fine lines marked her face, like the gentle handwriting of time. But her eyes—those eyes—still held the same quiet rebellion.

She turned, and the years collapsed.

"Ayaan," she said.

His name broke inside him. "Maya."

They walked through fog, through memory, through the echo of everything unsaid. She spoke of her two children, her small town, and her work as a school counsellor. He spoke of lectures, research, and the novels that never made it past chapter three.

They laughed at shared foolishness and fell silent at shared sorrow.

When they reached the ridge where they had once imagined futures they were too afraid to pursue, she sat down slowly.

"I used to think," she said, brushing frost from the bench, "that some people come into your life to teach you how to wait."

He exhaled, as though releasing a confession.

"I waited too," he said. "For timing. For courage. For… the right words."

"And they never came?" Her voice was gentle, carrying the weight of years.

"No," he said, his throat tight. "They lived inside me, but never found their way out."

Maya looked at him—not with anger, but with a quiet sadness that felt like snowfall: soft, inevitable.

"I needed to hear them, Ayaan. I hoped… hoped so much that you would say something. But life doesn't wait forever. Eventually, I had to move forward."

He swallowed. "I thought you understood."

"I did," she said. "But understanding is not the same as being chosen."

The wind stirred the oak leaves like pages turning.

At last, he spoke, his voice trembling.

"I loved you. From the moment you read Neruda with your eyes half-closed… I loved you. I just never learned how to be brave."

Her eyes filled—not with regret, but with a fragile tenderness.

"I loved you too," she whispered. "Quietly. Fiercely. But I needed more than almosts."

They laughed then—a broken, healing kind of laughter.

For a moment, the mountains stood silent, bearing witness to two people mourning a life they never lived.

"I imagined it sometimes," she said. "Our life. Mornings with shared coffee. Arguing over bookshelves. Children who looked like both of us. A home filled with too many books and too little logic."

"And I would have built that life," he said, "brick by trembling brick."

"But you didn't," she replied softly. "And now we belong elsewhere—to other people, other promises."

He nodded, the pain settling like frost.

"Then let me carry you quietly," he said. "In the spaces between my sentences. In the hush before sleep."

She blinked back tears. "And I'll carry you—in poems I never show anyone, in the spaces between heartbeats."

They stood.

Then came something he had not expected.

She reached into her bag and took out an old, yellowed envelope, its edges brittle with time.

"I found this last month," she said. "A letter I wrote to you—twenty-five years ago. I never sent it."

She placed it in his hand.

It was addressed to him.

Unopened.

A confession frozen in time.

"Read it," she whispered. "But not now. Not here."

Ayaan felt his breath catch.

No goodbye was spoken.

Because this was not a goodbye.

It was a return to a truth too late to live, but not too late to honour.

They walked in opposite directions—she toward the road, he toward the trail.

And in his coat pocket lay the letter.

A story unopened.

A word unspoken.

A love half-written.

Some loves—the deepest ones—are not meant to be lived.

Only remembered.

Only carried.

Only felt.

SECTION III
Women Who Rise

17

Of Eyes and Lips

The eyes often reveal what words cannot. Nanda's eyes were like that—brimming with laughter when she danced, soft with compassion when she witnessed suffering, and endlessly deep, as though they held the secrets of a universe. Yet her lips told a story she wished to forget. Born with a cleft lip, she had endured surgeries, whispers, and rejection. Though admired on stage as a dancer of rare versatility, she remained guarded in life, convinced that the world would never look beyond her flaw.

At nearly thirty-five, her mother's search for a suitable match had grown relentless, yet remained fruitless. Suitors turned away after a single meeting. The mask she wore in her studio, ostensibly for health reasons, was in truth a shield—a place of refuge. Still, Nanda nurtured a quiet longing: not just to be loved, but to be cherished for who she truly was.

Her dance school became a sanctuary for others. She opened its doors to young girls with disabilities—those with hearing loss, physical deformities, and scars of their own. She taught them that dance was not about perfection, but about freedom. In helping them overcome their inhibitions, Nanda found a deeper purpose in her own life.

One evening, after rehearsal, Aryan appeared. A photographer with an unusual gaze—his eyes drifting slightly due to a condition—stood at the studio door, camera in hand.

"I'd like to photograph you," he said simply. "I want the world to see your story."

Nanda offered a hesitant smile and asked, "Why me? I'm far from perfect."

Aryan shook his head. "Perfection is overrated. You dance as if you're telling the truth. That's what I want to capture."

What began as a project gradually grew into something more intimate. Through his lens, Nanda began to see herself differently. He focused not on her scar, but on her spirit—the grace of her movements, the depth in her eyes, the fire in her expression. In turn, her presence transformed his work. His portraits gained a depth he had never achieved before, as though she brought his art to life.

Nanda, too, came to understand Aryan's vulnerabilities. His drifting gaze had once made him a subject of ridicule, and his quietness was often mistaken for indifference. Yet she saw him clearly in ways others never had. Where others saw distraction, she saw intensity. Where others saw flaws, she saw strength.

They became mirrors to each other. He revealed the beauty she struggled to see, and she gave voice to the gentleness he kept hidden. Their bond was not about filling emptiness, but about amplifying light—like two incomplete notes blending into a perfect harmony.

One evening, after an emotionally charged performance, they found themselves in a rain-soaked café, the city blurred beyond the glass.

"You've changed how I see myself," Nanda whispered, her eyes glistening. "I thought my scars defined me. But with you, I feel… whole."

Aryan reached across the table and gently covered her trembling hands. "And I thought my gaze was a weakness. But you—" he smiled softly—"you've shown me a different way of seeing. You make me feel complete."

Their kiss that night was not merely an expression of affection, but a moment of recognition—the meeting of two souls who had longed to be truly seen.

Their story soon grew beyond them. Aryan's portrait series, *Unmasked,* was praised for its raw honesty and humanity. Nanda was invited to represent a global charity initiative, her journey symbolising resilience and acceptance. Standing on stage without her mask, surrounded by the very girls she had once inspired, she felt the applause envelop her like a blessing.

Yet beyond the recognition and accolades, what mattered most was the quiet sense of completeness they found in each other. In Aryan's gaze, she discovered reverence. In Nanda's laughter, he found light. They did not erase each other's scars—they honoured them.

For theirs was not a love built on fixing, but on acceptance; not on concealment, but on revelation. Together, they were not perfect—together, they were whole.

18

The Golden Cage

"I wish I could break
The intricate cage holding me back.
The misty mornings were so enchanting.
I, too, longed to feel the chill on my bare wings."

Sara left the message on her notepad, the page lying open and fluttering as if composing its own melody in the wind that streamed through the window, left open for the first time.

Her husband's home was beautiful, adorned like a bride—perhaps even more beautiful than the bride herself. That was Sara's first thought when she arrived at Ram Shukla's ancestral mansion in Kasauli, barely a day after their grand wedding.

The hill station was nothing like Mumbai. Gone were the blaring horns, the restless energy, and the liberating anonymity of city life. Here, the mist rolled over the mountains like a quiet spell—enchanting and suffocating at once.

Sara had met Ram at a crowded press conference at the Taj Palace. She was a young journalist, notebook in hand, when she noticed him across the room—charming, composed, untouched by the chaos of cameras and chatter. Their eyes met, and a fleeting smile passed between them like a secret. That single moment turned into coffee, then long conversations, and eventually a love that felt urgent and destined.

When Ram proposed, his confidence made her believe anything was possible: love across communities, across traditions, across the invisible boundaries families drew. "You'll never feel caged with me," he had promised once, brushing a strand of hair from her forehead.

She had believed him.

At first, the house dazzled her—towering verandas, antique chandeliers, a library lined with forgotten books. Every corner whispered of history. But soon, the beauty grew heavy. The air inside was thick with rules Sara had never agreed to.

"Don't wear that," Ram said one morning, folding away her bright kurti. "It's too loud for the wife of the Shukla family." His voice was soft, his smile gentle, but the command was unmistakable.

She laughed it off, telling herself it was just an adjustment—a compromise, the price of marriage. But gradually, the corrections multiplied: her clothes, her phone calls, even the way she laughed too loudly at dinner.

Once, when she teased him in front of his cousin, Ram's hand rested on her wrist beneath the table—not affectionate, not angry, but firm enough to remind her: stay in line.

Whenever Ram sensed her slipping away, he wrapped her in sudden tenderness. He would appear in the library with hot tea, kiss her forehead, and tell her how lucky he was to have her. He even booked tickets to her favourite band's concert on a whim, only to cancel them the next day with a casual, "Something important came up."

The cycle was dizzying—warmth one day, withdrawal the next.

Her writing, once her oxygen, became his favourite target. "These stories—why waste time? You're my wife now. Isn't that story enough?" he would say with a chuckle, though his eyes warned her not to argue.

And when she questioned him—softly, carefully—he twisted her words.

"I never said you couldn't call your family," he would insist, even as her phone lay locked in his desk drawer. "Why do you make me out to be controlling? You imagine too much."

She began to doubt herself. Was she overreacting? Had she misunderstood him? His calmness made her feel irrational, unstable, and foolish.

Months passed, and her world shrank to the walls of the gilded house. The mist outside her window became her only companion. She longed to walk through it, to feel its chill against her bare skin.

One evening, she gathered the courage to speak.

"Ram," she began gently, "I want to visit my family in Mumbai. Just for a few days."

His fork froze mid-air.

"Why?" he asked, his tone deceptively calm.

"Because I miss them. It's been months since the wedding."

His eyes hardened. "Your family is here now. What will people think if you run back so soon? They'll think you're unhappy."

But I am unhappy, she wanted to scream. Instead, she nodded, swallowing the truth like poison.

That night, she wrote furiously in her hidden notebook: I am disappearing, piece by piece. If I don't leave now, there will be nothing left of me.

The next confrontation came after one of her long walks in the hills.

"Where were you?" Ram asked, his voice clipped. "I called. You didn't answer."

"I must have missed it," Sara replied, her pulse racing.

His eyes narrowed. "This ends now. No more wandering. You're my wife—your loyalty is here."

Her voice trembled, but she stood her ground. "I'm your wife, Ram, but I am still myself. I won't live as your prisoner."

For a moment, he looked stunned. Then his face hardened. He stepped closer, his breath sour with rage.

"You ungrateful girl," he hissed. Before she could react, he spat on her. The warm sting on her cheek slid down like a mark she could not erase.

He turned and walked out, his footsteps deliberate, the front door slamming like a final decree.

Sara stood frozen, trembling. The taste of salt lingered on her lips. Something inside her broke—not loudly, but with the quiet certainty of a string stretched too far finally snapping.

That night, she did not sleep. She washed her face and packed a small bag—her secret journal, a change of clothes, a few pieces of jewellery. At dawn, while the house still slept, she stood at the door, her heart pounding.

She looked back once. The mansion gleamed in the morning light, as beautiful as ever.

It was a golden cage, nothing more.

The mist swirled around her as she stepped outside. It clung to her skin, cool and alive, whispering of freedom. She hesitated for only a moment, then moved forward—breathless, but unafraid.

Her wings, though heavy, began to stir.

And this time, she did not stop.

She walked into the mist—finally free.

19

A Light of Her Own

"When does the light appear the brightest?" Bhavna's voice was soft but steady, like a lamp shielding its flame in a wind-blown hallway.

She sat across from Shirin at the Brightman Mental Health Centre. The room was quiet, washed in pale blue light and cushioned silence. November pressed against the windows—dull skies and smudged smog. Shirin's breath was shallow; her asthma had flared, but it was not just her lungs that felt heavy. It was her heart. November always returned with a fog she could not shake.

She shifted in her chair and met Bhavna's eyes, uncertain. "I don't know… what do you mean?"

"Sometimes," Bhavna said, folding her hands in her lap, "we only notice the light when it breaks through our darkest hours."

Shirin lowered her gaze, her fingers tugging at the frayed cuff of her sweater. Clinical depression, anxiety, and survivor's guilt—those labels had followed her for nearly a decade. Therapy and medication helped, but November still arrived like a tidal wave, dragging her under. It was in November, ten years ago, that her father died, and she had never forgiven herself.

She had been nineteen—a brooding, brilliant girl with dreams too large for their cramped Mumbai apartment. She had just been shortlisted for an Everest Base Camp expedition, her childhood dream: scaling the Himalayas, breathing the sacred thin air, touching the edge of the world.

She had begged her father to let her go.

"It's just the Base Camp, Baba, not the summit," she had pleaded. "I can manage my asthma. I've trained for this. It's all I want."

Her father had shaken his head, gentle but resolute. "Not now, Shirin. Your mother is unwell. This isn't the time."

"But there'll never be a perfect time! Don't you see? I need this!"

He had made her tea and brought it to her room. "Your mother is ill, beta. You are needed here."

She had rolled her eyes. "You always say that. You want me to stay caged in this house like Ma."

He had placed a tender hand on her head. "I just want what's best for everyone—for you too."

But she had brushed his hand away and stormed out.

That was the last time they spoke.

She left for the expedition two days later—angry, unrelenting, desperate to prove herself. And while she stood among icy winds and prayer flags, trying to feel triumphant, her father collapsed while climbing the stairs to their third-floor apartment. It was a silent, sudden heart attack. No one was home.

Her phone had been out of network. She had been unreachable. By the time she returned and rushed to the hospital, he was already gone.

Her ailing mother had been outside the emergency room, clutching her husband's phone—her voice trembling, her eyes hollow. The light had gone out of her.

Shirin carried those moments like stones—her father's last look, her mother's unanswered calls, the missed messages. It had been too late. She believed she had killed him—with her absence, her anger, her ambition.

So she stopped moving, stopped dreaming. Her life froze at nineteen. Her mother's death soon after deepened her misery.

College became a blur. Friendships faded. Jobs came and went like smoke. She evaded success, responsibility, and any choice that resembled living—as though preserved in amber, embalmed in regret.

"Darkness isn't the enemy, Shirin," Bhavna had said during one of their first sessions. "It teaches us to appreciate the light. We don't have to fear it. We can learn to sit with it."

Her words stirred something dormant. Shirin closed her eyes and drifted into a memory—an old vacation at a beach in Kerala. Her father had held her hand as they watched the sun sink in a blaze of orange and red.

"The darker the night, the brighter the stars," he had whispered.

She had once believed he was magical. Now, she wondered if he had simply understood pain more deeply than she ever had.

"I guess that makes sense," she murmured. "But when you're in it, it feels endless. Like the darkness isn't just outside, but inside you."

"That's why we start small," Bhavna said. "Close your eyes. Imagine you're in a completely dark room. But there's one candle burning—just one. Can you see it?"

Shirin nodded slowly. The image flickered—a tiny golden flame holding back a sea of black.

"That candle is your resilience," Bhavna continued. "It might be small. It might waver. But it's there. It has survived everything—every storm, every November."

Shirin did not speak, but something loosened in her chest. She felt it—a flicker of warmth.

Later, walking home under a brooding sky, she let the cold wind brush her face. Diwali had passed, but the city still carried traces of celebration—sparklers on sidewalks, fairy lights drooping from balconies, half-burnt candles on stairwells. The air was heavy with lingering smoke, but now and then a sudden breeze cleared a patch of sky, revealing shy glimpses of blue.

Her apartment greeted her with silence—not peaceful, but blank. She made tea and stood by the window, cradling its warmth. Her fingers drifted to a drawer in the living room. She opened it and pulled out a single white candle, untouched since a power cut months ago.

She lit it.

The flame shimmered, uncertain, and then steadied. Shirin watched it as though it were breathing. It barely lit the room, but it shifted something within her. It was not enough to fix everything, but it was enough to remind her: she was still here.

That night, she wrote in her journal for the first time in months:

"Today I lit a candle. And for a moment, I felt okay. Maybe that's enough. Maybe okay is a good place to start."

Bhavna helped her go deeper.

"Let's talk about guilt," she said one morning. "What if your father never blamed you? What if he died loving you?"

Shirin cried then, long and unfiltered. She clutched a tissue and wept for the nineteen-year-old girl who had never learned how to carry grief.

Slowly, she began writing letters to her father—letters of apology, of love, and eventually, of forgiveness.

"I blamed myself so I wouldn't have to accept that I couldn't control everything," she once wrote. "But I see now that I was only a child. And you, Dad—you loved me still."

She lit a candle for every letter she wrote.

Bhavna nudged her forward. "What else brings light into your life?"

"I don't know. I haven't thought about it in years."

"Try," Bhavna said. "Let's make a list—not of goals or achievements, but of light: people, memories, sensations, even flavours."

They called it her "Light List." - The smell of Ma's chai on winter mornings; her niece's voice: "Miss you, Shiru Maasi!"; Pavement after rain; singing in the shower; fresh bedsheets; Baba's beach stories; the candle.

In December, Shirin began volunteering at an animal shelter. Once a month, she visited an old-age home, listening to stories that echoed her father's laughter.

In tiny pots, she planted herbs—lemongrass, basil, tulsi. She learned to make tea blends. One day, on a whim, she signed up for pottery.

"Something about shaping clay feels like rebuilding myself," she told Bhavna.

There was healing in service, joy in green sprigs, and power in creation.

Some nights remained hard. The darkness did not disappear entirely. She still had panic attacks. There were days when even noon felt too early to rise. Guilt still crept in, whispering the names of the gone.

But now, she met those nights with ritual.

On New Year's Eve, while the city buzzed with noise and celebration, Shirin stayed in. She wore her softest sweater, played her father's old ghazals, and lit seven candles in a row.

She whispered to them, one by one:

"Hope, breath, memory, grace, patience, forgiveness, me."

She was not cured.

But she was not broken either.

Somewhere between grief and growth, silence and song, solitude and service, Shirin began reclaiming her light. She was learning to sit with her shadows, to honour the quiet flame within, and to believe—truly believe—that she could be her own light.

And in doing so, she became something extraordinary— a lighthouse, not just for herself, but for others still lost at sea.

20

The Silence

"Distance weaves a silence between hearts, yet the deepest fear lies not in the stillness, but in wondering, does absence intensify longing, or does it gradually erode you from their soul?"

His every promise was hollow, his words felt like needles piercing bare skin, a bee sting to the heart. He always kept me away whenever I wanted to get closer.

Reasons and excuses were handy whenever I complained. I was branded a drama queen - Someone who demanded attention, someone who demanded respect, care, affection, and, more than anything, love! I guess it was more than what he could offer. It felt like I asked him for his entire world. In return, what I got was a perfectly measured dose of silence!

An eerie silence consumed me, like a bottomless void pulling me deeper into its relentless grasp, where even my own thoughts dissolved into oblivion. Why did he approve the match when Aunt Ratna proposed it? Why did he agree to marry me in the first place? What did he truly want from me? What had I done to deserve this deafening silence?

The questions were endless, yet no answers ever came. Even when his shirt carried the unmistakable scent of a woman's fragrance, even when lipstick stains whispered tales of betrayal, I endured it all. My suffering remained cloaked in silence.

I saw him laughing that day, with someone who looked like a princess, a young princess. He was laden with shopping bags – her shopping bags! So he used his one foot to swing the door open wide for the princess.

Another pang—his smile, wide and effortless, made the princess blush. I was taken aback by this gentleman, to whom I was married, who had never opened a door for me, even though I did his laundry, washed his dishes, and, all the more, made the bed where he slept—oblivious to the fact that there was another soul, with a beating heart, lying next to him.

I had wanted to freeze the moment and make myself believe he was capable of such chivalry, albeit for the princess.

Just an hour ago, we ended our call. He claimed to be in a city a few hundred miles away from our home. It was always work that created the distance, and the silence just filled the vacuum. He had ended the call, as always, abruptly.

He said, "It's going to be a demanding day, filled with meetings. I might not even have time to grab a bite."

Poor soul! Labouring for hours, even on our anniversary!

And yet, there he was, at Jacob Mall, the very place where couples spend their honeymoon days. In a quiet corner in Middletown, where tarot readers line the streets with their stalls, where lovers stroll hand in hand through narrow lanes, their paths cluttered with trinkets, fine antiques, woodwork, handicrafts, stoles, perfumes, and toys meant for lovers.

Yes, I came searching for one such trinket to gift him for our tenth anniversary. I was to give him a bigger surprise, too.

He was supposed to be in back-to-back meetings when I called an hour ago to remind him of something as trivial as our anniversary. I swallowed my words as he inundated me with tales of his work, how he was rushing from one cubicle to another, trying to get everything in order, how the market was chaotic, the buyouts massive, and so on. I do not remember him calling me by my pet name or even wishing me a happy anniversary. All I heard was profound silence and the jarring clatter of utensils in my mind.

I thought about the centrepiece on the dining table I had made. The gifts were to be arranged around it—ten of them, representing the years of silence I endured.

There were occasional moments of intimacy, for the need of procreation, where I was told I miserably failed. Ten years, and no little feet blessed my home. The silence overpowered every noise made on initial occasions, with its frequency increasing each passing year. The distance created a silence that was deafening to my soul.

As I stood there watching him, my mind churned with memories, realisations, and an unbearable ache that felt like it might consume me whole. The princess giggled as he brushed a stray lock of hair from her face, his touch so tender, so unfamiliar from the man I thought I knew. I clenched my fists, fighting the hot tears threatening to spill. But this time, the tears were not just of sadness; they carried something else: anger, clarity, and an unexpected surge of resolve.

I turned away, unable to watch anymore, and found myself walking aimlessly through the narrow lanes of the mall. My thoughts raced. For ten long years, I had waited, yearning for him to see me, to love and cherish me. I clung to the hope that he would abandon his indiscretions and choose loyalty. I had given him everything—my time, my dreams, my body, and my soul—only to be met with cold indifference and suffocating silence.

And now, with the harsh truth laid bare before me, I finally saw it—I had been chasing a mirage all along. I stopped in front of a small café and sank into a chair. The aroma of freshly brewed coffee filled the air, mingling with the soft hum of chatter around me. I pulled out my phone and stared at the screen. Our last call was still logged there, a stark reminder of his lies. My thumb hovered over his name, tempted to call him, to confront him, to scream and demand answers. But what would that change? Would it erase the years of neglect? Would it undo the betrayal I had just witnessed?

No, it would not. I slipped the phone back into my bag and reached for the small box holding the trinket I had bought for him. Opening it, I stared at the wooden heart, the engraved words mocking me: ***Forever yours***. I laughed bitterly. Forever? No, not anymore.

My thoughts shifted to the surprise I had planned for him – The one that had filled me with both excitement and dread for weeks. I had not told him yet, not even when I called earlier. I had wanted it to be special, to see the joy on his face when he found out. But now, as I sat in that café, I knew he did not deserve it. He did not deserve me.

The bigger surprise was life-changing. A baby! After years of heartbreak and self-doubt, the universe had finally gifted me the miracle I thought I would never have. I was three months along, and every flutter of excitement I had felt for the future was now tinged with bitterness. Could I raise this child in a home where silence suffocated love? Could I subject my baby to the same indifference I had endured for a decade?

The answer was clear. I could not.

Later that evening, I packed my bags. It was not impulsive; it was long overdue. As I stood by the door, I glanced at the framed photo of us on the wall. The smiling faces felt like strangers. I took it down, placed it face down on the table, and stepped out.

I did not know exactly where I was going, but I knew it was away from him, from the silence, from the life I had allowed myself to settle for. My hand instinctively rested on my stomach, and for the first time, I felt something close to hope.

This silence, I realised, was not the end. It was the beginning of a new chapter, a chapter where I would no longer wait for someone else to fill the void. I would create my own happiness, not just for me but for the life growing within me.

And as the sun rose higher, bathing the world in light, I stood tall, ready to embrace a future where the silence was not my enemy but my canvas—a space to write my own story, one filled with hope, resilience, and love.

I realised I was already deeply in love with the baby growing inside me. And I was ready to give back my husband, the silence he had gifted me all along.

He chose silence, and I chose freedom. The silence he embraced would now echo through his life, while mine would be filled with the music of laughter and love.

21

The Shattered Crown

Vishakha had long stopped expecting the world to celebrate her. Applause, she believed, belonged to younger women—those whose bodies had not been shaped by childbirth, whose faces were untouched by sleepless nights, and whose hair had not yet surrendered to streaks of grey.

These days, mirrors had become uncomfortable companions. They reflected not just softened skin and fine lines, but also years of sacrifice—years spent putting everyone else first, of dreams folded away and forgotten. Yet where praise had faded, purpose had taken root.

At *Anugraha,* the charitable foundation she had built from scratch, Vishakha was far more than a figurehead. She sat barefoot on cold cement floors, teaching women from the slums to trace the alphabet. She sorted through cartons of donated food, her sleeves rolled up, her kurta marked with sweat. She persuaded hard-nosed businessmen to part with their profits. She was grit, fire, and quiet rebellion in human form.

Still, on some nights, when silence pressed in around her, she wondered what it might feel like to be seen as beautiful again.

One afternoon, the chairperson of Anugraha leaned forward, her bangles clinking softly.

"Vishakha," she said, her eyes sparkling, "the Miss/Mrs. Vega Star pageant has opened registrations. It's a prestigious, widely covered platform. If you participate, Anugraha will gain visibility, sponsorship, and awareness. You are already the face of this cause—why not let the world see it?"

Vishakha laughed, a little embarrassed. "Me? On a stage with sequins and cameras? I'd rather spend that money feeding children than hiring stylists."

But the chairperson gently clasped her hand. "Sometimes, to fight for others, we must first confront our own doubts. You can be a symbol."

That night, Vishakha stood before her mirror longer than she had in years. The woman staring back no longer seemed like someone past her prime. She saw strength in her shoulders, resolve in her jawline and a quiet radiance in her eyes.

"I am still a queen," she whispered.

The next morning, she registered.

Rehearsals struck like a storm. Dressing rooms overflowed with satin and ambition. Heels clattered like war drums, and laughter rang sharp and rehearsed.

In her simple kurta, Vishakha felt like an outsider. Whispers circled the room.

"She doesn't belong here," someone muttered.

Alicia, the reigning favourite, made no effort to hide her disdain. Tall, poised, draped in couture, and surrounded by stylists, she was everything the cameras adored.

"This isn't a charity drive," Alicia said lightly, just loud enough to be heard. "It's a beauty pageant."

A ripple of laughter followed.

Vishakha remained composed. A faint smile touched her lips.

"You speak of one kind of beauty," she said calmly, her gaze steady. "I carry another."

Her words lingered in the air.

The talent round was her opportunity. She had prepared a monologue on women's empowerment, drawn from the stories of Anugraha.

But minutes before her turn, she opened her bag—only to find it empty. Not a single page remained, except for a torn scrap with a cruel message: *Let's see you shine now.*

A flicker of panic rose within her. Around her, a few smirks appeared, though no one could be held responsible.

Her hands trembled. Then she thought of the women she worked for—women who spoke their truths without scripts or microphones. If they could, so could she.

When her name was called, she stepped onto the stage. The spotlights blinded her, and silence pressed in. She took a deep breath.

And then, she spoke.

"Good evening.

Women's empowerment is not about perfection—it is about possibility. It is the courage to dream boldly, to speak confidently, and to rise after every fall. It is not one woman winning; it is all of us lifting each other higher.

Today's woman defines her beauty not by appearance, but by strength, compassion, and purpose. If standing here inspires even one girl to believe she is enough, capable, and deserving of her dreams, then that is my true victory.

Thank you."

Backstage, Vishakha exhaled. She had not just survived—she had risen beyond fear.

The evening gown round brought another challenge. The backstage area buzzed with chaos—dresses swishing, hairspray thick in the air, stylists rushing about.

Vishakha unzipped her garment bag. It was empty.

Her heart pounded as she searched frantically. Finally, behind a trunk, she found her gown—crumpled, sticky, and drenched in wine. The fabric was ruined.

A few giggles echoed nearby.

"What a tragedy," someone whispered.

For a moment, shame tightened her throat. Too old. Too plain. Out of place.

But then she remembered the women at Anugraha, who turned discarded fabric into something beautiful. If they could transform ruin into art, so could she.

"Scissors," she said firmly.

The dresser hesitated. "Ma'am?"

"Scissors. Please."

She worked quickly. Snip by snip, she reshaped the damaged gown—cutting the hem into an asymmetrical flare, twisting torn fabric into a sash, and crafting a bold headpiece. The wine stain spread across the satin like deliberate abstract art.

When she stood up, the mirror reflected not damage, but reinvention.

Onstage, the audience gasped. Whispers turned into astonishment. The judges leaned forward as applause filled the hall.

The final round—the question-and-answer segment—awaited. The question was simple: "What does beauty mean to you?"

One contestant answered first. "Beauty is youth, a perfect face, and a flawless figure." The judges seemed unimpressed.

When Vishakha stepped forward, her voice was soft, yet it carried across the room.

"Beauty is not symmetry or youth. It is resilience. It is the strength to bend without breaking, to wipe away tears and keep moving forward. It is kindness that gives without expectation, and courage that rises after every fall. Beauty is a fire—one that continues to glow even in the fiercest storm."

A deep silence followed. Then the hall erupted into a standing ovation.

The crown was hers.

Backstage, as she prepared for her victory walk, a sudden crash startled her. On the floor lay the crown—shattered into pieces.

For a moment, despair flickered. Then she bent down and gathered the fragments. Her hands trembled, but her voice was steady.

"They thought this would break me," she whispered. "But broken does not mean defeated."

She stepped onto the stage, holding the fragments high.

"Tonight, this broken crown tells a greater story than a perfect one ever could. Every woman has been told she isn't enough. Let these shards remind us—we rise stronger, brighter, and unbreakable."

The applause was thunderous.

Later, alone in her dressing room, Vishakha sat in quiet reflection. She thought of the women at Anugraha, and of the reflection she had once doubted—now radiant with confidence.

Down the corridor, Alicia stood before a mirror. Her flawless image stared back, yet something within her felt hollow.

"Why wasn't I enough?" she whispered.

Days later, a package arrived at Vishakha's home. Inside was a crown of gold, studded with diamonds.

The sender: Tanishq Jewellery.

A note read: *For the woman who proved that the strongest gems are forged under pressure.*

Along with it came a contract—an offer to become their brand ambassador—and a donation of one crore rupees to build *Anugraha's* new education centre.

Vishakha placed the crown on her head, not because she needed it, but because she no longer did.

Her victory had never been about titles or jewels. It was about proving—to herself and to women everywhere—that even broken crowns can shine. And so can they.

SECTION IV

Strange Worlds & Hidden Doors

22

The Red Button

It was an ungodly hour, suspended between night's last breath and dawn's reluctant yawn, when Shubhendu Bose glanced at the clock. Only three hours remained before the quarterly board meeting, where both the company's future and his reputation as one of India's sharpest corporate strategists would be decided. He had even less time before the deadline set by his publisher for a manuscript tied to his other identity—the celebrated novelist whose books sold in the millions, dissecting human ambition and betrayal with surgical precision.

The corporate honcho in him urged him to shut the laptop, rehearse the merger pitch, and refine the legal arguments to impress the board. The novelist in him, however, remained transfixed by the blinking cursor of the unfinished manuscript—restless, hungry. For months, he had sculpted this story from bone and shadow: a murder mystery steeped in lies and laced with betrayal. Yet the conclusion remained elusive, stubbornly refusing to take shape.

He rubbed his eyes. Words blurred into one another like blood dissolving in water. His mouth tasted of stale coffee and desperation. He needed clarity—or perhaps escape.

The apartment exhaled silence as Shubhendu left his desk. Even the walls seemed asleep, lulled by the hush that descends when the world pauses. He padded barefoot into the living room, where moonlight slanted through the blinds like broken prison bars. Everything felt familiar—until it didn't.

On the centre table, resting atop a thick, timeworn tome he did not remember owning, sat a glowing red button.

He froze. His skin prickled. The button glistened—too vivid, too theatrical—like a fresh wound in a black-and-white photograph. He had not placed it there. He had never seen it before.

Beneath it, carved into a wooden plaque with unsettling precision, were the words:

"Press it, if you dare."

The CEO in him scoffed. Nonsense. A prank? A hallucination? Corporate training had taught him to assess risk and demand data before making decisions. He imagined his board colleagues—their tailored suits and guarded expressions. If they saw him hesitate over a glowing button, they would deem him irrational, unfit for leadership.

But the novelist in him leaned closer. Every story begins with a dare. Every ending demands a leap. The button was not merely an object; it was a metaphor, a plot twist offered by unseen forces.

He felt his two selves circling, colliding—the rational strategist calculating consequences, the feverish writer craving narrative inevitability.

It was a test, perhaps, or a story waiting to be written.

Shubhendu pressed it.

Click.

The sound cracked through the silence, sharp as a whip. The air folded inward. The room twisted, groaned. His breath hitched as a vortex tore into existence before him, its centre a spinning gyre of impossible geometry. Colours he had no names for pulsed within it.

The businessman inside him screamed of risk, liability, and damage control. The writer whispered of destiny, climax, and catharsis.

He stepped through.

It felt as though he were being unravelled and rewritten. He emerged into a void that was anything but empty. Stars blinked like ancient eyes. Nebulae swirled in slow motion. The space itself felt conscious.

Then, suspended before him like a theatre screen in an astral dome, his novel unfolded.

His characters moved, breathed, killed, and wept. He watched them betray and be betrayed. Every plot point he had written flickered with luminous, terrifying precision.

And then came the climax—the ending that had eluded him like a fugitive always just out of reach.

He saw it—perfect, inevitable, devastating.

His hand flew to his pocket. No pen. No paper. But his gaze caught a familiar glimmer in the void: the red button again, still glowing, still whispering—

"Press it, if you dare."

The corporate leader in him would have paused, negotiated, and calculated the cost of action. The novelist did not hesitate. He pressed it again.

The stars fractured. The cosmos collapsed inward like a dying lung. He was hurled back through the void, limbs stretched across realities—until—Thud.

Shubhendu lay sprawled on his living room floor. The vortex was gone. The button had vanished and the book, too. His heart thundered.

But he remembered the ending. God, he remembered it.

He staggered to his desk, feverish with purpose. Words poured out of him, as if his fingers were mere conduits for something beyond. He wrote like a man possessed—like the young writer who once stayed awake through hostel nights, scribbling stories on scraps of paper. Yet beneath the rhythm of his keystrokes, he heard the ticking clock of the boardroom, the faint echo of corporate destiny awaiting him. His two lives converged on the page.

Just as the final sentence appeared on the screen, a shrill alarm rang.

He was in bed.

The sun had risen—harsh and unforgiving. His sheets were tangled around him like restraints. His desk stood clean. There was no manuscript, no coffee mug, no blinking cursor, only the sterile stillness of an untouched morning.

Had he dreamed it?

The CEO in him searched for logic. Was it a stress-induced hallucination or the result of exhaustion? The novelist in him trembled. No dream leaves impressions this sharp. He rubbed his temples. He could still hear the button's click, still see its red glow.

Then he noticed a single page resting on his bedside table, its ink still fresh.

It was the last chapter, the very words he remembered writing. And yet, he had not written them here. He had not typed a thing since the previous night.

His breath caught. The ending was flawless—too flawless.

He turned the page over.

At the bottom, in blood-red ink, were the words:

"Every ending has its price. Yours has just begun."

23

Through the Looking Glass

Swagata Raman, a woman with thirty-something wisdom (okay, forty-five, but who's counting?), lived in the heart of Chennai, a city that never seemed to sleep—not because of glamorous nightlife, but because of honking that could rival a rock concert, roadside vendors who believed shouting was the best sales pitch, and the children downstairs practising their eternal symphony: "screech toy, fling toy, scream at toy."

She often felt like a lone goldfish trapped in an aquarium filled with enthusiastic families—parents with two kids, three board games, and four thousand photos uploaded to Instagram every weekend. Swagata's life, much like the traffic outside her balcony, felt like it was going nowhere... only getting louder.

Her daily routine was as thrilling as watching coconut chutney ferment. She had an MBA from a prestigious college, had landed a "cushy" job that looked wonderful on LinkedIn, and spent her weekdays trapped in fluorescent offices where the tube lights flickered more than her motivation. On paper, she was successful. In reality, the job drained her spirit faster than her morning coffee flowed through her veins. Her life was predictable and unchanging—a merry-go-round where the horse was made of emails, meetings, and PowerPoint slides with pie charts nobody cared about.

But what stung more than the boredom was the comparison. In her apartment building, she was the only one without children to chase, homework to supervise, or vacation plans to obsess over. Everyone else was living what she mockingly called the "Instagram Life": husbands and wives posing with kids in coordinated clothes, hosting game nights and holding Monopoly boards like trophies, beaming under fairy lights. Swagata's Friday nights, meanwhile, were spent on her couch, watching Netflix with a packet of chips. Her "wild social calendar" consisted of scrolling through Instagram and muttering things like, "Oh, look, Priya and family are in Bali again." Didn't we all vote them "Most Likely to Vacation Forever"?

One evening, after yet another soul-sucking day of pretending to care about quarterly reports, Swagata gave in to a colleague's invitation to a concert. It was not her kind of music. Honestly, she could not tell the difference between a jazz riff and a guitar solo. But the energy in the hall was contagious.

As the bass thudded in her chest and the crowd swayed in unison, something in her woke up. For once, it felt like adrenaline—not caffeine—was coursing through her veins. The music was not background noise; it was freedom—loud, unapologetic, and alive. For a fleeting moment, Swagata believed she could be someone else—someone dazzling, someone magnetic, someone unshackled from corporate drudgery and her lonely one-bedroom apartment.

That night, still buzzing, she stood in front of her mirror. Her reflection stared back: slightly messy hair, tired eyes, and delivery-pizza arguments etched into her frown lines. But this time, something was different. The edges of the mirror shimmered, as though someone had spilt stardust along the frame.

Was it an optical illusion or too much concert adrenaline? She wondered. Still, her hand lifted almost involuntarily. When her fingertip touched the glass, a jolt surged through her body—something between a lightning strike and that gut-dropping moment when you realise you have left your phone in a cab.

And then, poof!

Gone were the beige bedroom walls and the hum of her refrigerator. Instead, Swagata stood under blinding neon lights, a microphone in hand, while thousands of fans chanted, "Swagata! Swagata!"

She looked down and nearly fainted. She was wearing a sequined jumpsuit that sparkled brighter than Marina Beach at sunset. She was no longer Swagata, the bored corporate worker. She was a pop diva, basking in roaring applause.

The rush was intoxicating. Every clap filled her veins with fire. This was it, she thought. This was what she was meant for. But then, the noise stretched into something hollow. The stage lights burned her eyes, backstage buzzed with strangers whose names she did not know, and when she tried to laugh, it echoed oddly, as if she were cheering in an empty room.

The thrill soured in no time. Fame, she realised, was like cheap candy—a sugar high that left you queasy.

She bolted backstage and found a mirror propped against a wall. Desperately, she touched it, and in a blink, she was back in her apartment, staring at her tired, potato-like reflection.

But now she knew: this was no ordinary looking glass. It was a portal. Each touch catapulted her into another life.

One day, she found herself in a high-rise corner office, playing the role of a powerful CEO. Her name was embossed on the mahogany desk; subordinates scurried around her like nervous ants. "Ma'am, your speech for the shareholders is ready," someone said, handing her a thick sheaf of papers.

She cleared her throat, tried to channel gravitas, and promptly tripped over the words "diversified portfolio." The room fell silent, cameras clicked, and investors whispered. Swagata gulped and muttered, "Why does this sound like Greek mixed with Sanskrit?" Someone coughed politely. The illusion cracked. She was not commanding respect; she was a child trying on her mother's heels.

Frustrated, she touched the mirror again.

The next time, she landed in the middle of a TED Talk stage. The red circle glowed beneath her feet. The screen behind her read: "The Future of the Global Economy." A packed audience leaned forward, ready to be inspired.

Swagata blinked and thought: *Global economy? I struggle with my monthly credit card bill.*

"Ladies and gentlemen," she began, "the world economy is... uh... like biryani. You think it's simple rice until you realise there are too many masalas hidden inside."

The crowd chuckled, thinking it was a metaphor. Emboldened, she rambled on, mixing GDP with turmeric and foreign trade with sambar powder. The applause at the end was thunderous, but Swagata knew the truth: she was a fraud in borrowed brilliance.

Again, she fled to the mirror.

The adventures became addictive—a fashion runway, a safari in Africa, a wilderness survival test. But the thrill wore off faster each time, leaving her emptier. She was not running to new worlds; she was running from herself.

Finally, half-joking, she thought: Why not space?

In a blink, she was weightless, floating among galaxies that glittered like spilt diamonds. The Earth curved in the distance, blue and fragile. For the first time, the silence was absolute—no honking, no chatter, no Netflix autoplay, just her, suspended in eternity.

At first, it was breathtaking. But soon, loneliness pressed down harder than gravity. There was no one to laugh with, no coffee to share, and no simple human voice to tether her. She whispered into the void, and her words vanished. The thrill collapsed into an ache.

After what felt like months, or maybe years, she stumbled upon a cracked, dusty mirror in the corner of a deserted space station. Her hands trembled as she touched it. In an instant, Chennai's familiar skyline returned, bathed in the golden light of evening.

Swagata collapsed onto her couch, breathless but changed. The mirror had not just shown her other worlds; it had forced her to face her own hunger to be someone else. She had chased glamour, power, brilliance, even infinity—but none of it filled the void.

Now she understood: her life did not need to be perfect to be worth living. It needed to be hers.

With a small, wry smile, she pulled out her phone, snapped a photo of the mirror, and uploaded it to OLX with the caption: "One magical mirror for sale. Transports you anywhere—except to the life you actually need to live."

Then she closed her eyes and listened to the familiar screech of kids below her balcony. For the first time, it did not sound like chaos. It sounded like life.

And this time, it felt enough.

24

The Poovar Conspiracy

In the coastal village near Poovar, the sea was more than a vast expanse of water. It was a living, breathing entity, a companion to those who understood its rhythms. To Vasu, it was both a sanctuary and an obsession.

Born to a fisherman and a school teacher, he grew up in a home where books and boats coexisted. His mother, an ardent believer in education, had nurtured his love for knowledge, while his father had taught him the silent language of the waves. Unlike other children who built sandcastles and played in the tide, Vasu would sit for hours by the shore, watching the sea breathe, its ebb and flow a lullaby that shaped his dreams.

But it was the mangroves that held his deepest fascination. Their labyrinthine roots and salt-resistant leaves whispered secrets of resilience and survival. It was among these ancient trees that Vasu first discovered *Avicennia Marina,* an unassuming species that he believed contained properties powerful enough to reverse genetic disorders.

Despite financial struggles, he pursued his passion, enrolling in a PhD program in marine biology. To sustain himself, he worked as a boatman at dawn and dusk, ferrying tourists through the mangrove-lined waterways. His weathered motorboat doubled as his floating laboratory, where he meticulously recorded observations, sketched plant structures, and conducted preliminary extractions.

Beneath his scientific fervour lay a quiet yearning: to leave behind more than just footprints in the wet sand. He dreamed of recognition, of proving that something as unassuming as a mangrove leaf could change the course of medicine.

What he did not know was that someone else had been watching, someone who saw in his discovery an opportunity that stretched far beyond research.

One evening, as the Poovar sky blazed with hues of tangerine and violet, a motorboat docked at the jetty, carrying a group of well-dressed tourists. Among them was a woman draped in a deep red saree with a golden border, her dark hair cascading over her shoulders like liquid night.

She introduced herself as Setulakshmi.

She claimed to be a teacher, though there was an air of solitude about her, a certain wistfulness in her eyes that spoke of something deeper, something unspoken.

Vasu, accustomed to tourists who marvelled at the scenery but cared little for its deeper mysteries, was intrigued. There was something about her gaze, the way she lingered on the mangroves that suggested she was not just there for the views.

Perhaps, like him, she was searching for something.

The journey through the mangrove-fringed waters was serene, the sun casting golden ripples on the surface. Vasu, as always, spoke with reverence about the ecosystem, about the intricate balance that allowed life to thrive in these brackish waters.

Setulakshmi listened with rare attentiveness.

"These trees," she mused, running her fingers lightly along the wooden railing of the boat, "they adapt to both the land and the sea. It's poetic."

Vasu smiled, surprised by her choice of words. "Poetic, yes, and practical. Their roots filter salt, allowing them to survive where other plants cannot."

She tilted her head, as if absorbing not just his words but something beyond them. "And your research—what exactly do you hope to find?"

It was an innocent question. And yet, something in the way she asked it made him hesitate.

Still, the way she looked at him, the way her voice carried genuine curiosity, made him lower his guard.

"If my theory is correct," he said, "the compounds in their leaves can help repair damaged DNA. It can change the way we treat genetic disorders."

Setulakshmi's lips parted slightly, her fingers tightening around the railing. "That would be extraordinary."

There was something in her voice, an urgency, a personal stake, that made him wonder.

But he did not ask. Not yet.

Over the next few days, Setulakshmi returned.

At first, it seemed incidental. She would linger at the jetty, waiting for an opportunity to ask another question, to listen a little longer. But soon, it became clear that she was drawn to more than just the science.

She watched him as he worked. Her presence was like a quiet shadow in his world.

One evening, as the waves lapped gently against the shore, she sat beside him on his boat, the scent of salt and wet earth mingling with the faint perfume she wore.

"You said the extraction process is delicate," she said softly. "Can you show me?"

Vasu hesitated, but there was something disarming about her, the way she looked at him, as if he alone held the answers to questions she had spent a lifetime asking.

And so, under the golden glow of a lantern, he explained. He spoke of timing, of the careful balance between heat and salinity, of how one misstep could render the compound useless.

She listened with rapt attention, her fingers brushing his as she reached for a vial.

"You trust me, don't you?" she whispered.

Vasu exhaled slowly. "I want to."

And for a moment, he let himself believe she was there for him. Not just for the knowledge he held.

The explosion was so huge that it tore through the silence.

One moment, the boat rocked gently with the tide; the next, fire and debris filled the air, and Vasu was thrown into the sea.

The salt water burned his lungs as he struggled to surface, his vision blurred by smoke and pain.

Through the chaos, he saw her.

Setulakshmi.

She was not running. She was not screaming.

She was watching from the shore.

And then she was gone.

Vasu survived. But he was unconscious.

When Vasu finally gained consciousness, his body felt like a cage of broken reeds. The hospital ceiling above him was a dull yellow, trembling in and out of focus. Someone had lit incense; its sharp sweetness clashed with the antiseptic air. He tried to speak, but only salt and smoke lingered on his tongue.

"They say you're lucky," the nurse murmured, adjusting the IV line with the practised motion of someone who had seen many versions of luck. "The boat exploded. You could've died."

He blinked, and fragments flooded back - The lantern, the vial, Setulakshmi's fingers brushing his, the sudden roar of fire, and then the sea claiming him with both arms.

But what haunted him was not the explosion; it was the stillness on her face as she watched him drown.

The police asked their questions. They photographed the wreckage. They shrugged. It was easier to blame faulty machinery than intentional sabotage. Only fishermen came by to offer sympathy, speaking of bad omens and angry tides.

But Vasu knew better.

He found the fuel line first—cleanly slit, deliberate, then the missing notebook and then the realisation that the lantern had not fallen by accident.

The betrayal was total.

He returned to the mangroves not as a scientist, but as a wounded animal. The roots whispered and filtered and continued their quiet alchemy, indifferent to the cruelty of humans.

There, among the Avicennia Marina, he buried what was left of the man who once believed curiosity was enough to protect him.

Months became years in the way shorelines erode—one forgotten grain at a time.

The explosion stripped him not only of his research but also of his credibility. Grants were denied. His advisor suggested he consider "adjacent careers." One panellist at a conference in Kochi patted him on the back and said, "Interesting theory, but without data it's just a story, Vasu."

Stories did not cure genetic disorders.

But exile sometimes creates opportunity. A visiting German biologist—Dr. Neukamm—heard him speak at a modest regional symposium and lingered afterwards.

"You speak like a man who has lost everything," she said in crisp English, "which makes you very dangerous to mediocrity. Come to Hamburg. Work with us."

It was not salvation. But it was motion.

And motion, after stagnation, felt like resurrection.

Germany was cold in the way science could be cold—precise, unsentimental, exacting. But the laboratories were well funded, the freezers were full, and the equipment was state-of-the-art. His work no longer happened on a weathered motorboat; it happened in sterile rooms humming with machines that cost more than entire fishing villages.

He rebuilt his research, not from memory, but from obsession. He worked through nights, ignored holidays, lived on coffee and nostalgia for mangroves that did not exist in Europe.

The first breakthrough was minor. The second, less so. By the third, journals began replying with interest instead of rejection. The compound extraction that once required lanterns and saltwater baths now danced between centrifuges and controlled heat cycles.

Still, he told no one about Setulakshmi.

And then one evening, while preparing a presentation for a medical congress in Zurich, his colleague handed him a journal.

"You should read this," she said. "Someone is finally catching up to you."

The headline hit him like a rogue tide:

A New Frontier in Gene Repair

By Dr. Ania Hussain

His eyes scanned the abstract, then the methodology. There it was—the very leaf he once held out to a woman in a red saree – The same hypothesis, the same biochemical pathway, even the salinity tolerance notes.

His pulse thundered.

She had not just stolen his research.

She had finished it.

She was being hailed as a pioneer.

For a long time, Vasu sat alone in that quiet laboratory, the journal trembling in his hands. He wondered if she remembered him, if she thought he had died that night, if the sea had delivered her everything she wanted and demanded nothing in return.

But the ocean never gives without taking.

When the Zurich conference announced she would be the keynote speaker, Vasu submitted his abstract with the calm precision of a man sharpening a blade.

He did not sleep the night before the conference. Instead, he watched old videos of Poovar—mangroves swaying like ancient guardians, fishermen calling out to one another across the water. He missed their simplicity, their unspoken truths.

At dawn, he buttoned his blazer, combed his hair, and walked into the auditorium.

The room filled with applause as Dr. Ania Hussain stepped onto the stage—poised, polished, celebrated. Cameras flashed, journalists scribbled, and investors leaned forward.

She spoke of breakthroughs, of genetic repair, of hope.

But she did not speak of lanterns or mangrove leaves or the man she left burning on a boat.

When the applause thundered, Vasu did not clap.

The tide had finally turned.

And this time, he would not drown.

Vasu did not wait for the conference to end.

The moment Ania Hussain—Setulakshmi—stepped down from the stage, he followed her.

She moved with practised ease, her elegant heels clicking against the marble floor, acknowledging a few people with polite nods, but never lingering. She could feel his eyes on her. She knew.

Vasu quickened his pace.

"Dr. Ania Hussain," he called out, his voice cutting through the hum of conversations.

She froze, just for a fraction of a second.

Then she turned, her face an unreadable mask. "I'm afraid I don't—"

"You do," he said sharply. "We have unfinished business, Setulakshmi."

Her breath hitched. It was the name she had long buried under accolades and reinvention, the name that had once belonged to a woman who had seduced, deceived, and destroyed.

And now, that past had caught up with her.

"I don't know what you're talking about," she said smoothly, clutching her designer handbag as if it were a shield.

Vasu stepped closer. "Oh, you do. And you're running out of places to hide."

Her eyes darted around—too many people. She would not risk a confrontation there.

Without another word, she turned on her heel and walked briskly toward the exit.

Vasu followed her.

She reached the parking lot, fumbled with her keys, and slid into a sleek black Sedan. The engine roared to life.

But so did he.

Vasu jumped into his car and followed as she sped past the city streets, weaving through traffic with the same calculated precision with which she had orchestrated his ruin.

The chase was relentless, until finally, she turned into a gated property and rolled to a stop in a quiet, upscale neighbourhood.

She was home.

Vasu parked at a distance, watching as she stepped out, her shoulders tense, her breath still uneven from the chase.

And then came a soft voice – "Mama!"

A little girl, no older than six or seven, wheeled toward her, her tiny arms outstretched. Behind her stood an elderly woman—the nanny, perhaps—who had been pushing the wheelchair but now stepped aside as Setulakshmi… no, Ania… took over.

Vasu's grip on the steering wheel slackened.

She bent down, whispering something to the child, her hands tender as she adjusted the shawl over the girl's frail shoulders.

Gone was the ruthless woman who had once walked away from a burning boat. Gone was the cold-blooded traitor who had shattered his world.

What remained was a mother.

She wheeled her daughter inside, her silhouette framed by the setting golden sun.

Something melted inside him - The bitterness of betrayal, the fire of revenge.

It all collapsed into a deep, cool ocean—just like the Neyyar river finally meeting the Arabian Sea through Poovar.

Had he been the estuary?

He was neither fresh nor salt, neither revenge nor forgiveness, Just something in between, something inevitable, something vast.

25

The Christmas Game[1]

The snowstorm had a sense of humour.

It began the very minute Miranda and Jason Smith checked into the Blue Pine Resort in Aspen—three full days before anyone else was due to arrive.

Christmas Eve fell on a Saturday, and the entire Smith family was expected by Sunday to celebrate both Christmas and Emily Smith's graduation on Monday. Emily was earning her master's degree in psychology and would soon leave for Europe for research.

Europe meant distance—distance from home, and from her parents' crumbling marriage, which had long been held together only by routine and pretence.

"Three days early," Miranda muttered, staring out the frosted window. "We could have been home finishing Christmas shopping. But no, we had to rush to Aspen for Emily's graduation next week."

Jason set down the suitcases, unfazed. "You said, 'Let's not be late for Emily's big day.' I took initiative. You used to like that about me."

"I used to like a lot of things about you," she murmured.

The heater hummed. The snow fell.

And the silence between them was older than the storm itself.

---

[1] First published in an anthology 'Tis the season to be jolly' by Nyra Publishers

They were there for their daughter—and, though neither would say it aloud, for what would likely be their last trip together before signing divorce papers in January, except Emily had other plans.

The highlight of the first day was a long power outage.

The lights flickered and then went out.

Jason groaned. "Seriously? I paid extra for the 'mountain view suite,' not the 'cave experience.'"

Miranda's phone flashlight caught something on the mantel—a small envelope.

Inside, it read:

Welcome to the Blue Ridge Christmas Game!

Couples compete in fun daily tasks until Christmas Day. The winning pair earns a private cottage in the woods.

Santa is watching—always watching.

Round 1: Share the story of how you met. No skipping details.

Miranda exhaled, "Emily."

Jason chuckled, "Our daughter, the evil genius."

Still, they sat by the fire, two mugs of cocoa between them, and began the game.

"Fine," Miranda said. "We met at that ridiculous college debate. You were arguing against Shakespeare."

"I wasn't against Shakespeare," Jason protested. "I was against mandatory Shakespeare. There's a difference."

"You called *Hamlet* overrated."

"I still stand by that."

She smiled despite herself. "Then you spilt coffee all over my notes."

"Strategic move. I figured if I ruined your notes, you'd talk to me."

She laughed—a sound neither of them had heard from her in weeks. "That's what you call flirting?"

"It worked, didn't it?"

They both fell quiet, remembering that first winter—cheap coffee, crowded libraries, nights spent arguing about poetry and politics, making up with laughter.

For a few moments, the storm outside became nothing more than background music.

The highlight of the second day was confessions.

Another envelope appeared in the morning. The power was still out. The Wi-Fi was dead. There was just the two of them—and the game.

Round 2: Confess one thing you never said.

Miranda hesitated. "You go first."

Jason rubbed his neck. "I never told you I was terrified when we bought our first house. I acted confident, but I couldn't sleep for days. I didn't want you to think I was scared."

She smiled softly. "You always wanted to look strong. Even when your car broke down, and you tried fixing it with a spoon."

Jason grinned, "Your turn."

Miranda's voice dropped. "I never told you I felt lonely—even when you were right there. You stopped talking to me—not out of anger, just indifference. That's worse."

The words settled between them, heavy as the snow outside.

Jason reached out and tucked a strand of hair behind her ear, a gesture that felt both familiar and foreign.

"I didn't stop caring," he said quietly. "I just didn't know how to fix things anymore."

"Neither did I," she whispered.

And somewhere in that silence, the first crack appeared in the wall they had built around each other.

The highlight of the third day was the pillow war.

Round 3: Recreate one funny fight.

Miranda raised an eyebrow. "Funny? Which of our fights ever qualified as funny?"

Jason grinned, "The one with the pillows."

Before she could react, a pillow hit her square in the face.

"Jason!"

"You said recreate!"

Feathers exploded mid-air, laughter echoing through the room as they mock-fought like teenagers. Breathless, they collapsed onto the couch, surrounded by white feathers that looked suspiciously like snowflakes.

"I can't believe you once stormed out over a burnt lasagna," Miranda said, still laughing.

Jason chuckled. "In my defence, you told me I was useless as a husband and a cook in the same sentence."

"You were both that night."

"But I ordered pizza."

"That was the redeeming part."

Then came the quieter memories—long nights with sick children, missed anniversaries, lost weekends.

And the day they lost Lily, fifteen Christmases ago.

Miranda's voice trembled. "You shut down after that. I did too. But instead of reaching for each other, we just drifted."

Jason's eyes glistened. "Every Christmas since, I've woken up thinking of her—and of you. But I didn't know how to hold you without breaking."

They did not speak again for a long while. They simply sat side by side, as they used to with Lily, watching the snow fall.

The fourth day brought a blizzard, trapping them together.

No electricity, no phones, just another envelope.

Round 4: What made you stay this long?

Miranda stared at it thoughtfully.

"You first," Jason said.

She sighed, "Your ridiculous optimism. You believed every bad day could be fixed with pancakes. You never gave up on anything—except us, toward the end."

He smiled faintly. "And you—your fire. You'd argue with the television if it were wrong. You made the house feel alive. Even when we fought, I knew I was lucky."

They laughed again—truly laughed—at the absurdity of it all: her perfectionism, his carelessness, her labelling every jar in the fridge, his inability to ever close a drawer.

The things that once annoyed them were, they realised, the things they missed most.

It was love—disguised, unspoken, stubborn—but still there.

Christmas Eve

When the blizzard finally lifted, Aspen glowed under a blanket of white.

On their breakfast tray lay the final envelope:

Final Round: Make a wish for each other.

Miranda smiled. "You go first."

Jason said softly, "I wish you'd never doubt how much I love you, even when I'm too foolish to show it."

Her voice cracked. "I wish we'd remember that marriage isn't about staying perfect—it's about staying."

They needed no more words. The kiss was clumsy and familiar—two people finding their way back after twenty-five winters of love and loss.

Just then, the door burst open.

"Surprise!" Emily laughed, snow-dusted and radiant.

"The family's here! Merry Christmas!"

Jason grinned. "You little mastermind."

Miranda said, half-teasing, half-grateful, "You planned this, didn't you?"

Emily shrugged. "I just gave you the space. You did the rest."

And she was right.

The storm had not trapped them. It had freed them.

That night, as carols filled the air and cocoa warmed their hands, Jason leaned close.

"Same time next Christmas?"

Miranda smiled and said, "Only if you promise to burn the lasagna again."

They laughed, clinked their mugs, and watched the snow fall—soft, endless, forgiving.

Because love, like Christmas, always finds its way home—even after the longest winter.

26

The Bio-Nuclear Project

Lutopia was a town built on secrets. Beneath its polished streets and manicured parks, a legacy of whispers slithered through the shadows—whispers of a classified experiment that had once shaken global intelligence networks. Years ago, rumours circulated about a revolutionary bio-nuclear weapon tested on the uninhabited outskirts of the town. Then came silence. The project vanished as abruptly as it had appeared, buried beneath layers of governmental denial. But the people of Lutopia had long memories, and behind every curtain, suspicion flickered like static.

Steve Mallory and Ryan Quinn were master's students at the local university—brilliant minds bound by ambition. Steve, a theoretical physicist, was obsessed with unlocking the secrets of subatomic anomalies. Ryan, a visionary biologist, dreamed of bioengineering a cure for cancer. Though their disciplines differed, their curiosity converged on an experimental thesis that merged particle physics with genetic manipulation—an ambitious exploration of bio-nuclear fusion.

On the eve of spring break, their project hit a snag. They needed more liquid nitrogen to stabilise their cooling array. Ryan suggested a quick trip to the campus warehouse, and Steve, though exhausted, agreed. The roads were deserted under the town's steel-grey twilight.

That was when they saw him.

An elderly man, gaunt and trembling, stood alone by the roadside. His coat was patched, and his shoes seemed to belong to another century. Compassion overruled caution, and they offered him a ride. He accepted, his voice a whisper of gratitude, and asked to be dropped off at a house near the warehouse.

The mansion, upon their arrival, looked like something torn from a forgotten century—an architectural relic shrouded in ivy and silence. Intrigued by its strangeness and the old man's cryptic demeanour, they followed him inside for what he promised would be "the best hot chocolate on this side of reality."

What greeted them was no kitchen.

The house was a technological mausoleum, its corridors lined with dormant machinery and biometric locks. Blueprints lay scattered like confetti across steel workbenches, and a subtle vibration thrummed beneath their feet. The old man led them down a dim hallway to a chamber containing an Olympic-sized pool. Its surface was smooth as obsidian, reflecting no light—it absorbed it.

"Look closely," the old man murmured.

They leaned in. At that very moment, the lights went out.

A sudden, brutal force hurled them into the pool. Panic surged as the water writhed into a whirlpool of impossible depth. They were dragged through a tunnel beneath the surface, their senses disoriented and lungs burning for air. Just as unconsciousness threatened to claim them, they broke through the surface—inside a transparent, tubular elevator descending through molten rock.

The walls pulsed red with the glow of magma, yet the interior remained icy and climate-controlled. The contradiction was deeply unsettling.

The capsule halted. From the shadows emerged a nightmare.

The creature was humanoid only in outline. One half of its face bore a glowing, unblinking eye; the other was a grotesque fusion of machinery and flesh—aperture-like nostrils and a lipless mouth twitching with coded signals. Its skin was plated with antiquated technology: cellular panels, retractable antennae, and humming circuits.

It pressed a device on its wrist, sending the elevator upward with Steve still inside. Then it turned and opened a vault door.

Beyond lay a vast chamber bathed in sterile white light. Rows upon rows of hospital beds stretched into the distance. Bodies lay motionless beneath sheets, their stillness too precise to be natural. The creature tapped its wrist again, and a dozen more beings emerged, each uniquely colored and equally horrifying.

Ryan broke first. He ran blindly and crashed into a cryo-storage unit, sending it toppling to the floor. Preserved human organs spilt out like grotesque fruit, and blood splattered across his shoes.

Steve, paralysed, began to understand. This was not entirely Earth. The facility existed between realms, built with technologies that defied comprehension. The magma powered it, the nitrogen cooled its experiments, and the figures in the beds—perhaps human—were test subjects.

The creatures were neither fully alien nor human. They were hybrids, part machine and part flesh—living proof of the very bio-nuclear fusion Steve and Ryan had theorised.

Ryan stumbled into a chamber marked with a radioactive symbol. In desperation, he pulled an emergency lever.

A blinding burst of radiation erupted.

The creatures collapsed instantly. Systems overloaded, and sirens wailed. The elevator plummeted back down, and Steve leapt inside just as a secondary explosion tore through the subterranean complex. The shockwave hurled ash and twisted metal in every direction. Through the glass, Steve saw Ryan—burning, disintegrating, consumed.

The capsule shot upward. Steve blacked out.

When he regained consciousness, he was lying on the cold floor of the warehouse, a nitrogen cylinder clutched to his chest. A professor was calling his name, and paramedics crowded around him. But Steve could not speak—not a word. The trauma had fractured his mind.

At the hospital, his silence persisted. Psychiatrists diagnosed him with catatonia. He drifted in and out of awareness, unable to distinguish reality from nightmare.

Then, two nights later, his hospital door creaked open.

Ryan stood there.

Only it was not Ryan.

His posture was too rigid, his expression devoid of emotion. His eyes glinted with the same chilling bioluminescence Steve had seen in the creature's singular eye. Strapped to his wrist was the control band from the underground lab.

Before Steve could react, Ryan crossed the room in eerie silence and injected a syringe into his temple. Agony surged through his body like liquid lightning. His muscles seized, and his vision fractured into static.

As his consciousness faded, Steve understood the truth.

Ryan had not survived.

He had been assimilated, repurposed.

Steve felt his memories unravel, his sense of self peeling away like old paint. The band was scanning him now—recording, replicating. He was next.

And far beneath the town of Lutopia, something ancient and artificial stirred awake once more.

The project had never ended.

It had only just begun.

27

Journey to Freedomland

"Fasten your seatbelts!" Captain Batra boomed, sounding somewhere between a pilot and a motivational speaker at a government workshop. His ATR-42 sliced through the clouds like a paper plane on steroids.

"You are about to touch down in one of the most incredible destinations in the world," he declared, as though they were landing in Switzerland rather than a mysterious place called Freedomland.

On board were 45 freshly appointed government recruits—not "fresh" like mint leaves, but new to the system. They were the chosen ones, titled Freedom Executive Officers, trained to untangle red tape rather than add to it. Their destination was not a training hall with broken microphones and watery chai, but the fabled Freedomland—an immersive, transformative boot camp where the ideals of liberty and governance were not just discussed, but lived.

From the windows, the recruits squinted at landscapes so meticulously planned that it seemed almost suspicious. Transparent government offices—where transparency was not just a policy buzzword—stood alongside parks laid out with geometric precision, and traffic flowed with astonishing smoothness. One officer muttered, "This must be CGI."

The plane landed. A brisk breeze greeted them, faintly scented with accountability. On the tarmac, guides stood with grand titles such as Expert in Human Rights and Specialist in Participatory Governance. Adjusting their oversized government-issue blazers, the recruits braced themselves for two days that promised to be anything but ordinary.

Their first stop was Liberty Square, dominated by a towering statue of a hand releasing a dove. "Finally, a monument where pigeons aren't sitting on us," someone joked. Citizens thronged the square, engaging in heated debates before calmly casting votes on digital tablets.

This was democracy with Wi-Fi, where even a teenager's rant about potholes was logged, debated, and resolved without waiting for three election cycles. The recruits were stunned. Was this what governance looked like without adjournments, walkouts, and sensational news debates?

Next came the Hall of Rights, a museum so vivid that it made history textbooks seem lifeless. Gandhi and Mandela engaged in holographic debates, while Rosa Parks glared at anyone who dared sit in her seat. Freedom here was not a dusty chapter—it was a living reminder that real people had struggled, sacrificed, and stood firm so others could stand tall.

A rare silence followed as the recruits exited. For once, even the most talkative among them had nothing to say.

As night fell, they entered Unity Park, a vibrant carnival of coexistence. Muslims broke bread with Hindus, North Indians danced to Carnatic rhythms, and Tamilians taught Punjabis how to eat dosa without forks. It was loud, chaotic, and imperfect—and yet, it worked.

Here, they learned the most radical truth: freedom was not about building walls around identities. It was about opening doors—sometimes even your kitchen doors—to those who saw the world differently.

By dawn, they were ushered into the Innovation Hub, alive with youthful energy. Here, freedom wore hoodies and built apps. Teams brainstormed solutions to corruption, unemployment, and even the persistent mystery of why every government form asked for a father's name but rarely a mother's.

One group designed solar-powered buses. Another proposed AI-driven ration system. A particularly daring officer suggested "Mondays without meetings"—an idea bold enough to spark near rebellion.

Finally, they entered the Chamber of Reflection, a space so quiet it made libraries seem noisy. Each recruit was asked to write their personal vision of freedom. Some wrote about fearless speech, others about justice, and a few about uninterrupted Wi-Fi.

But beneath their words, a common theme emerged: freedom was not about "me," but about "we."

As the plane ascended from Freedomland, Captain Batra's voice returned, softer now.

"What you've seen is not a fantasy. It is a possibility. The challenge is not to admire it here, but to build it out there."

The recruits sat upright. They were no longer just officers returning from training—they carried with them an uncomfortable awareness that freedom did not end with independence movements or grand speeches. It lived in everyday choices: signing a file without expecting a bribe, allowing dissenting voices to be heard, or fixing a pothole before it claimed another scooter.

This is because in the end, freedom was never just about breaking chains. It was about refusing to forge new ones.

And as the plane disappeared into the clouds, each recruit carried back not just training notes, but a quiet promise—to become everyday freedom fighters in offices, streets, and villages, long after the applause had faded.

SECTION V
Endings That Begin Again

28

In Every Life, in Every Way

Mira stood at the edge of the old bookstore, a gentle drizzle misting her scarf as twilight dipped the city in gold and red. The alley was the same—narrow, cobblestoned, stitched with creeping vines and secrets. Yet it felt slightly altered, as if reality had bent just enough to let the past breathe through its cracks.

She was not sure why her steps had led her there. It was a place she had not seen in years—perhaps lifetimes. Maybe it was the wind whispering her name, or the scent of old paper calling her home. Something invisible, yet deeply familiar, pulled at her like a forgotten lullaby drifting through dreams.

The wooden signboard still hung above the entrance, its letters faded but proud: *Timeless Tales*. The 'T' swayed gently in the breeze, as if waving at her. As she stepped inside, the door let out a soft creak—a sigh of welcome. The air was thick with the scent of yellowing pages, ink, and time, like memories pressed between paragraphs.

Shelves stood like ancient sentinels, their spines etched with titles and secrets. Dust danced in the dim amber light like tiny spirits. Mira moved slowly, as if afraid of waking ghosts. Her fingertips brushed the books, each one stirring a flicker of déjà vu. Her heart began to quicken, beating in a rhythm that defied logic. It felt like listening to a song she had never heard, yet somehow knew by heart.

She turned into the poetry section.

And there, he stood.

His back was to her, his figure silhouetted by fading light streaming through a stained-glass window. He was reading from a thin book, holding its pages as if they were sacred. The gentle curve of his jaw, the curl of dark hair at his collar—something about him struck her like lightning in slow motion.

Then he turned.

Time paused.

Their eyes met, and the world fell silent. Somewhere, a bell chimed. Somewhere, a page turned.

He blinked, confusion flickering across his face. "I… I know that this sounds odd, but… have we met before?"

Mira's voice was barely a breath. She replied, "Maybe not here. Maybe not now."

He let out a soft, hesitant laugh, almost reverent. "This poem I'm reading says something like that—about love finding its way back, about souls meeting again, even as strangers."

Mira stepped closer, her heart pounding as if it remembered something her mind did not. Her eyes fell on the page he held open: *Every Version of Forever.*

"Even if names change. Even if we forget," she whispered.

He looked down at the page, then back at her. "You know it?"

"I wrote it," she said.

For a long moment, he simply stared. Then, slowly, as if dawn had risen within him, a smile spread across his face.

"I'm Parthsarathi," he said, holding out his hand.

"Mira," she replied, her fingers meeting his like a secret handshake from another life.

They stood amid the hush of forgotten books, something ancient stirring gently between them. Neither spoke of the pull in their chests, the echo of a dream they could not name, or the sense that the universe had shifted to bring them together.

They did not need to.

That night, they shared coffee in a candlelit café that seemed to exist only for them. Rain tapped softly against the windows like a blessing. They exchanged stories, though they did not feel like stories—they felt like memories.

Mira spoke of poetry, of how words sometimes came to her in sleep, how her lines often felt dictated by something unseen. Parthsarathi spoke of his travels, of wandering through cities that felt strangely familiar—places he had never visited, yet somehow knew.

"Sometimes I think I'm chasing someone I already know," he said, stirring his cup absently.

Mira wrapped her fingers around her own cup. "Maybe you are."

There was laughter too—light, unexpected. He teased her for scribbling verses on napkins; she teased him for ordering coffee so sweet it could pass for dessert. These small details settled between them like anchors, grounding them in something real.

A few weeks later, Parthsarathi vanished.

His phone went dead. His emails bounced back with cryptic errors. Mira returned to the bookstore, only to find it empty and boarded up. An old man sweeping the alley insisted there had never been a bookstore there, not in the twenty years he had lived nearby.

Even the slim poetry book Parthsarathi had held was missing from her shelf, though she clearly remembered bringing it home.

At first, Mira thought grief had deceived her, conjuring a man out of longing. But one night, as she flipped through her journal, she found a short poem written in a hand that was not hers:

If I vanish, don't chase the wind
Find me in pages where verses begin.

Her breath caught. She clutched the journal to her chest, torn between heartbreak and awe.

Months later, at a literary symposium in Prague, Mira wandered into an exhibit of forgotten poets. Among faded photographs and vintage books, her pulse faltered.

There he was—Parthsarathi. Or rather, Krishna Rao, identified as a rising Indian poet who had vanished during a Himalayan expedition in 1979.

The face was the same—only younger.

Her knees weakened, and she gripped the glass display case for support. He had the same jawline, the same eyes that seemed to hold centuries. She whispered his name, but the room swallowed the sound.

For hours afterwards, she drifted through the city like someone unmoored. Questions stormed her mind. Had she stepped into a story unknowingly? Had time folded in on itself? Or was she destined to encounter fragments of him across lifetimes?

Back in her hotel, her trembling hands opened the journal again. The poem remained, the ink untouched.

In the years that followed, Mira searched—not just for him, but for others like her. And she found them.

A violinist in Vienna who dreamt of a woman for months, only to see her one morning on a train platform; A painter in Buenos Aires who repeatedly painted the same face, believing it belonged to a stranger—until she walked into his gallery and recognised herself on the canvas.

Mira began collecting these stories, weaving them into a book titled *Souls Between Lifetimes*. Critics expected scepticism, but the book became a phenomenon. Letters poured in from readers describing impossible encounters, inexplicable recognitions, and love that defied reason.

And still, on quiet nights, Mira wrote poems only he would understand.

Years later, on a rain-laced spring evening in Kyoto, she wandered into the ancient hilltop temple of Kiyomizu-dera.

Lanterns swayed like suspended fireflies, casting soft golden halos over cherry blossoms drifting gently in the breeze.

The air carried thousands of whispered wishes, folded into paper prayers tied to sacred strings. Bells chimed faintly in the mist, echoing like a forgotten song.

Mira stood beneath the falling petals, feeling the earth breathe beneath her feet. The air shimmered, as though time itself had thinned.

And then—he appeared.

Not from a path, nor from shadow, but as if formed from mist itself.

His eyes held the depth of oceans, his presence both familiar and distant, as though he had walked across centuries to find her.

"I knew you would find me again," he said.

She did not ask where he had been. She did not question whether he was real.

She simply reached for his hand.

And this time, he did not vanish.

They walked the temple grounds in silence, past moss-covered stones and still ponds that reflected starlight before it touched the sky. Beneath a wooden gate, he kissed her forehead like a promise remembered across lifetimes. Time bent gently around them, as if the universe itself bowed in reverence.

Years later, Mira sat wrapped in a woollen shawl on her porch, her granddaughter beside her. The child, eyes wide with wonder, asked, "How did you know he was the one?"

Mira smiled, soft and certain and replied, "Because even when we were strangers, my soul remembered him. Love like ours doesn't begin or end in one lifetime. It simply waits—in poems, in doorways, in cherry blossom breezes."

And in that quiet dusk, the child felt it—the tremor of something magical, the truth hidden in fairy tales, the eternity contained within a single glance.

Because some hearts, no matter how many lifetimes they wander, always find their way back to every version of forever.

29

The Sunday Breakfast

She woke up late. Binge-watching Netflix series on Saturday night had become something of a ritual. The morning sun spilt across the room, careless and golden, making the crumpled blanket look like a chaotic piece of art. She stretched, tucking the sheet around herself like armour.

"I should make breakfast," she murmured, though part of her still longed to curl back under the covers and remain in the stillness.

"Or," he replied, his voice gravelly with sleep as he sat up behind her and wrapped his arms around her waist, "we could order in. Or…" He pressed a kiss to her shoulder, "Skip breakfast entirely."

She laughed, startled by the lightness of it.

"You'd survive on Swiggy deliveries if it were up to you."

"Correction," he said, mock-seriously, "I would thrive on Swiggy and Zomato deliveries. I am a connoisseur of fine cardboard boxes and ketchup packets."

She shook her head, smiling despite herself. "Well, today your gourmet taste buds are getting scrambled eggs."

"Then the noble knight shall serve his queen," he declared, slipping off the bed with unnecessary drama.

The kitchen came alive with their presence—awkward movements, teasing remarks, clinks and clangs. He opened cupboards with great purpose, only to discover sugar where he was certain the salt should be.

"It's playing hide-and-seek," he muttered.

"Or maybe you just don't look properly," she teased, cracking eggs into a bowl.

He picked up the whisk like a sword. "Stand back, madam. This is where I shine."

She raised an eyebrow. "Gently. We're making breakfast, not a cyclone."

But of course, he whisked with such vigour that some of the egg sloshed onto the counter.

She groaned. "You're cleaning that."

"Worth it for the artistry," he grinned, clearly delighted with himself.

And somewhere between the whisking, the chopping, and her sighs of exaggerated despair, something unspoken shifted, because once upon a time, mornings had been very different.

She remembered them too well—the heavy silence of an empty kitchen, the way she would sit at the table with a mug of coffee that grew cold between her palms because no one was there to drink the second cup, the sound of the clock ticking louder than her heartbeat, the loneliness of scrambled eggs eaten quickly, mechanically, without joy.

Back then, mornings were something to survive.

Now, as she stirred the pan and he slipped behind her, his arms circling her waist, his chin resting on her shoulder, she felt the ache of the past dissolve into something softer. His breath brushed her neck—warm, grounding.

Healing had never looked better.

Not loud. Not dramatic.

But quiet.

Steady.

Sometimes, even silly.

Like sunlight creeping in through half-drawn curtains.

Like laughter spilling over unevenly chopped onions.

Like a man declaring her cooking worthy of Michelin stars when all she had made was eggs.

They finally sat down at the table, plates in front of them. He took a dramatic bite and widened his eyes.

"Unbelievable. Honestly, this is art, pure art. If Gordon Ramsay ate this, he'd retire."

She laughed, rolling her eyes. "You'd eat burnt toast and call it art if I made it."

"Exactly," he said without hesitation. "It's called loyalty."

And she laughed harder—laughed until her eyes watered, until her chest felt lighter than it had in years. In that laughter, she realised she was reclaiming the part of herself she thought had been buried under grief and loneliness.

He poured her coffee—two teaspoons of sugar, a splash of milk—the way he knew by heart. She watched him.

Love, she thought, did not always roar.

Sometimes it just chuckled in a messy kitchen.

Sometimes it tasted like scrambled eggs.

Sometimes it meant someone holding you steady while you learned to breathe again.

And for her, that was more than enough.

It was everything.

30

The Personal Diary

Mallika Venugopal wandered through the rain-glazed lanes of Pune like a poem trapped in human form. At forty-six, her elegance remained untouched. Her sarees were always handwoven, her *bindis* perfectly matched, and her voice calm, laced with literary metaphors. She taught creative writing at a local college and hosted intimate poetry salons on weekends. Yet, something intangible had shifted within her.

It began with small lapses—misplaced words, jumbled names. At first, it seemed amusing; then it grew unsettling. One morning, she found herself standing in her kitchen, staring at a boiling kettle, unable to remember why she was there. She misplaced her phone in the freezer. She forgot her best friend Rina's birthday—something she had never missed in two decades. The laughter with which she brushed these incidents aside began to sound hollow.

"It's just perimenopause with dramatic flair," she joked to her friends, though her voice cracked. The real rupture came when she looked at a framed photograph of her mother and drew a blank—not just the name, but the face, the warmth, the memory—everything vanished into a terrifying silence.

Behind her composed exterior, anxiety brewed. She began carrying sticky notes with reminders: "Check the stove." "Lock the doors." "Call Rohit." Her world, once an elegant dance of words, slowly dissolved into a fog of forgetfulness.

The neurologist's office felt oppressively bright. The hum of fluorescent lights grated on her nerves. Dr Vernekar, a middle-aged man with compassionate eyes and a clinical tone, tapped her MRI scans as though indicating a sinking ship.

"Early-onset frontotemporal dementia," he said, enunciating each syllable like a death knell. "It affects language, memory, and behaviour. It progresses quickly."

"How long do I have?"

"Perhaps six months before significant deterioration. A year, if you're fortunate. There's no cure."

The room seemed to tilt. The walls closed in. Her memories—her life—felt as though they were being auctioned to oblivion. She thought of her mother's humming voice, the smell of naphthalene in her sarees, Aarav's laughter in Paris, the night Siddharth read Neruda aloud to her. All of it was now on borrowed time.

"What can I do?" she asked, her voice barely above a whisper.

"Document, record, preserve. Create a diary of who you are before you forget who that is."

She stepped out of the hospital into a sunlit courtyard, the air heavy in her lungs. Yet an idea was already taking shape—a way to hold on to herself.

The next morning, she called Rohit Verma.

Rohit had been a quiet constant in her life. They had met twelve years earlier at the Jaipur Literature Festival. While others had fawned over her readings, Rohit had waited silently. "Your words feel like my past life," he had said, and she still remembered the quickening of her pulse.

A documentary filmmaker, Rohit was observant, empathetic, and remarkably patient. They had never been lovers, yet their bond carried depth and tenderness.

"I need you to do something for me," she said as they sipped tea on her balcony, surrounded by potted ferns and tinkling wind chimes.

"Anything," he replied.

"I need you to be my diary."

He looked at her, puzzled. "Your… diary?"

"I'm losing myself, Rohit. I need you to help me remember—not just facts, but feelings, moments, the texture of my life."

He nodded slowly, the weight of her request settling in. From that day on, every evening she recited memories to him: her first stage play in college, her first crush, her tumultuous affair with Aarav—the sculptor who had once sculpted her and gifted it to her—the stolen kisses with Siddharth at India Gate, the time she wrote poetry while waiting on a railway platform after a cancelled train during a college trip.

Rohit recorded everything—audio files, handwritten notes, and photographs pinned along timelines. But something within him stirred uneasily. There was no mention of him in her stories—nothing beyond friendship. Only a friend that was all he had ever been. The thought carried a faint sting of betrayal.

In truth, he had loved her quietly for years. Now that he had become the keeper of her memories, temptation took root.

At first, the distortions were subtle.

"Do you remember the trip to Lonavala?" he asked one evening. "You slipped on the cobblestones."

She frowned. "Wasn't that with Aarav?"

"No," he said gently. "It was with me. You were wearing that mustard scarf. We had bhutta by the lake."

She hesitated. She could almost see the scarf, taste the corn, feel the moment—but she could not place him there.

As her trust in him deepened and her mind dimmed, Rohit began altering more. He inserted himself into her past—into trips, gestures, and intimate moments. He reshaped Siddharth into someone cruel and Aarav into someone indifferent, planting the idea that they had always hurt her.

In his version of her life, he had always been her solace, her anchor—her only constant.

Her disoriented mind clung to these narratives. Yet somewhere deep within, a quiet resistance lingered—a whisper that something was not right.

Years earlier, during a three-month writing retreat in Coonoor, Mallika had begun an audio diary—one she kept secret, even from Rohit.

"I don't trust ink," she had once said to herself with a smile. "I trust voices."

She recorded her stories, thoughts, and raw emotions, hiding them like treasures throughout her home—inside hollowed-out books, beneath floorboards, even within tea canisters. She called it Project Shadow.

One afternoon, while dusting her shelves, she knocked over a copy of Sylvia Plath. A small recorder slipped out. She pressed play.

"This is Mallika. If you're listening, it means you're forgetting. And someone may be lying to you."

It was her own voice—warning her.

A shiver ran down her spine.

Over the following weeks, she uncovered more recordings—each one contradicting Rohit's version of her past: her romance with Aarav in Montmartre, Siddharth's handwritten sonnets, and Meher—her brilliant student who called her a second mother and once gifted her a rose quartz pendant "for courage."

She began to play along with Rohit, all the while reclaiming the truth from the shadows.

One evening, over dinner, she asked, "Tell me about my fortieth birthday."

"You didn't like the party," he replied. "We stayed in and watched films."

She quietly played a file titled *Bali_40_Birthday*. It was filled with her laughter, the crackle of a bonfire, and Aarav's voice whispering, "You are the storm I never saw coming."

Rohit fell silent.

She looked at him, her expression cold and steady. "You rewrote my life."

"I just... I loved you. I didn't want you to forget us."

"There was never an 'us,' Rohit."

With that, she closed the door on him.

Mallika then contacted Meher, now a tech prodigy based in Berlin. Meher had once been an orphan, supported through Mallika's charity work with the CRY organisation, and had always considered her a guiding force. She arrived within days.

Together, they created Echo—an AI-powered memory bank. Mallika poured everything she had into it: poems, photographs, voice recordings, writings, scanned letters—her entire lived experience. Echo built a personalised interface that allowed her to retrieve memories through symbols and phrases.

"Frangipani Dreams" unlocked summer recollections. "Hibiscus Red" brought back her college protest days. "Rain Tea" summoned Aarav's Paris apartment.

Echo did not merely store memories—it restored her.

Though her decline continued, slow and inevitable, Echo became her anchor. She forgot her cat's name. She once wandered into traffic. Meher became her caregiver, gently guiding her back with whispered reminders.

Yet whenever Echo played *Kala Ghoda 2009*, her face would light up.

"I remember love not by its heat," she would murmur, "but by the smoke it leaves behind."

Each memory became a ritual—a way back to herself.

They moved to Panchgani, to a quiet wooden cottage where the wind rustled through trees and silence offered comfort.

She forgot days, then names, then faces. But she never forgot poetry.

On her final morning, she looked at Meher and whispered, "Remember for me."

And then she was gone.

A year later, *Echo: A Diary Against Oblivion* was published. It became a literary sensation—a testament to memory, identity, and the dangers of manipulation.

The foreword, written shakily in her own hand, read: "To the woman I used to be—this is your resurrection."

At her funeral, Meher discovered a sealed envelope from Rohit. Inside was a letter: "I loved you. I feared your forgetting would erase me. So I rewrote you. I was wrong."

Enclosed was his falsified diary. Meher threw it into the fire.

The real story had already been told—in Mallika's own voice – A story of how she fought, and won, against all odds.

Epilogue

Stories do not end on the last page. They wait.

They follow you into silence, rise in moments you least expect, and whisper truths you did not know you were ready to hear. What you have read are not conclusions, but echoes of love that survived, of loss that transformed, of lives altered in the smallest, most irreversible ways.

If something stirred, unsettled, or stayed with you, then the story has already crossed over.

The book may close.

The echoes do not.